THE SHY GUY

NICOLA MARSH

Reclusive children's author Bo Bradford is on a tight deadline and the last thing he needs is a new illustrator barging into his orderly world and turning it upside down. Being a number one bestselling author means everything to him and he won't allow a bubbly, sassy illustrator to disrupt his goal, no matter how badly he wants her.

Tahnee Lewis falls for Wally the Wombat like the rest of Australia, but when she lands the dream job of illustrating Bo's incredible books she doesn't expect to find him as recalcitrant as his creations. She has two weeks to make the most of this once in a lifetime opportunity and if she can have a little fun along the way with the hot writer, so be it.

But when she finds herself falling for the hermit author, will she be able to walk away?

Copyright © Nicola Marsh 2022
Published by Parlance Press 2022

All the characters, names, places and incidents in this book have no existence outside the imagination of the author and have no relation whatsoever to anyone bearing the same name or names and are used fictitiously. They're not distantly inspired by any individual known or unknown to the author and all the incidents in the book are pure invention. Any resemblance to actual events, locales, or persons, living or dead, is coincidental.

All rights reserved including the right of reproduction in any form. The text or any part of the publication may not be reproduced or transmitted in any form without the written permission of the publisher.

The author acknowledges the copyrighted or trademarked status and trademark owners of the word marks mentioned in this work of fiction.

First Published by Harlequin Enterprises in 2007 as TWO WEEK MISTRESS
World English Rights Copyright © 2021 Nicola Marsh

One

Wally the wombat waddled out of his burrow into the sunshine and blinked. He was having a bad day. His friend Mandy the mole had upped and left him after getting married. No, this wouldn't do at all. He had to find a new friend to help him dig all day. Fast.

Bo Bradford's blog.

"How cute is that?"

Tahnee Lewis looked up from the computer screen and rolled her eyes at her sister Carissa. "You think that's cute? Wait until you see the pictures I come up with to dazzle the elusive Bo Bradford with."

Carissa smiled and slid onto the ergonomic chair next to her. "I have no doubt you'll dazzle this guy and become world famous and probably never speak to me ever again. But what I want to know is does he use Wally as a substitute for himself? His blog posts are cute but kind of sad too."

Tahnee shrugged, her gaze drawn back to the screen with

its colourful graphics and quirky animal drawings—which, to her critical and purely objective eye, weren't a patch on what she could produce.

"I have no idea. That's why I did an online search and this blog is all I can come up with, along with the requisite social media profiles, but no photos. His website is limited to a backlist of books and a brief bio without a pic."

"Don't most authors have photos on their websites at least? For promotional purposes?"

"Uh-huh, so his reclusiveness makes the elusive Mr. Bradford all the more intriguing."

When starting out in the publishing business, Tahnee would've given her best charcoals to work for a guy like Bo Bradford: Australia's number one children's author, with every book he penned a certifiable winner. His reputation hadn't dimmed in the last five years since he'd been published and though she could hold her own as an illustrator, she knew working with him would guarantee her work for life.

"You're actually going to live with this guy for two weeks?" A small frown creased Carissa's brow, the same frown she wore when her step-daughter Molly got into mischief. "And you know nothing about him?"

"Relax. My publisher put me in touch with his agent who organised the whole thing. Bo's on the up and up. I'll be living in a semi-detached flat attached to his place and this arrangement is going to be a win-win for both of us. He needs a new illustrator, I need a new job. And if all goes well, he'll hire me on a permanent basis."

Boy, did she need a new job. She was so close to achieving her lifelong dream, and having her publisher go under wouldn't deter her. She needed the money now more than ever.

Carissa's frown didn't disappear. "Yeah, but what's with having you live-in? The guy could be some sort of weirdo."

The same thought had crossed Tahnee's mind but the publishing world was small and she'd asked a few discreet questions, more than satisfied with the answers that the mysterious Bo Bradford was legit.

"He writes children's books." Tahnee rolled her eyes. "Do you see Wally having some kind of strange S&M fetish?"

Carissa's concerned gaze flicked to the PC screen and her frown vanished. "Good point. I guess a guy who spends his days creating cute little critters like Wally the Wombat can't be all bad."

"Exactly. Now, do you want to help me pack?"

"Like it's going to take you long to pack five pairs of jeans, your oldest denim jacket and the few tops you throw on under it."

Tahnee stood and placed a hand on her hip, thrusting out a leg clad in her favourite dark denim. "Are you trying to tell me something about my wardrobe?"

Carissa grinned. "Only the same thing I've been trying to tell you since we reunited and I could finally give sisterly advice."

"Let me guess. Not all men are attracted to denim?" She waggled her finger under Carissa's nose. "I've got news for you. The guys I date like it just fine."

"Right. And your last date was when?"

Okay, so her know-it-all, disgustingly-happy sister had a point. It had been a while since Tahnee had dated. Ten months to be exact. Not that she was counting or anything.

"All I'm trying to say is you don't know anything about this guy so it mightn't hurt to pack a few extras." Carissa's blue eyes glazed over in that dreamy, romantic haze she usually reserved for talking about her husband Brody, the single dad neighbour who'd taken one look at her sister and turned into a marshmallow. "Who knows? He might expect you to dress up for dinner?"

Tahnee laughed and shook her head. "What century are you living in? Girl, you've turned into a total sap since you got married."

"Nothing wrong with wanting my sister to be happy," Carissa said, the goofy grin on her face matching the gleam in her eyes.

"You're so right. I'll make sure all the single girls in Stockton know you're on the warpath."

Carissa chuckled. "You always need to have the last word."

"Too right. Now, I have a few hundred pairs of jeans that need folding so want to help?"

Carissa threw a cushion at her and she ducked, knowing she'd miss this even for a fortnight. Discovering her sisters Carissa and Kristen eight years earlier—after they'd been separated as youngsters following the death of their parents and adopted out to different families—had been surreal and getting reacquainted with her sisters had been a blast. Since meeting Carissa they'd been virtually inseparable. Until big, bad Brody came on the scene and her sister turned into a soppy romantic, though thankfully she still saw a lot of Carissa and her adorable kids, Molly and Jack, her six-month bundle of joy.

Family and friends were important to Tahnee, security more so, and she'd do anything to preserve it, including living with an eccentric stranger for two weeks in the hope to secure a stellar reputation in her field for the rest of her career.

Yeah, she could do this.

Two weeks in Sydney would be a breeze and winning over the reclusive Bo Bradford her number one priority.

And if he turned out to be a psycho, she'd stab him with her sharpest pencil.

Bo Bradford hated technology.

He hated wasting precious hours on updating his blog daily all in the name of promotion.

He hated telephones breaking his concentration and social media notifications interrupting his thought processes.

And he especially hated the damn intercom signalling the arrival of his replacement illustrator.

He clasped his fingers and stretched forwards to ease the kinks in his neck from staring at the computer too long, then pushed away from his desk and headed for the elaborate intercom system he'd had installed five years earlier when protecting his privacy became all important.

Stabbing at the talk button, he said, "Yes?"

"Tahnee Lewis here, reporting for duty."

Bo reared back from the intercom as if the woman had stuck her finger through it and poked him in the eye. She had a sense of humour? Great. He didn't need a comedienne, he needed a gun illustrator, and though she'd come highly recommended—and he liked what he'd seen of her work for a rival publishing firm—he believed in the old motto 'seeing is believing.'

Hitting the talk button again, he muttered, "Drive through. I'll meet you round the back."

"Right-o. See you in a sec."

Static crackled for several seconds and he realised he hadn't moved, something in the woman's voice captivating his attention. She sounded young. Too young. He needed an expert, not someone to babysit, and the faster he filled Moira's position the better.

Tahnee Lewis also had a tone, a challenging hint of insubordination he didn't like. She made it sound like he'd told her to come in a secret entrance reserved for disreputable folk, when he used the back entrance all the time because it led into the kitchen and family room, the most welcoming and lived in parts of the house.

He shouldn't make snap judgements, but ever since Moira had upped and left him in the lurch—okay, so his quiet illustrator may have had the longest engagement in history and had warned him she'd be out of here once the wedding ring slipped on her finger—he'd been floundering.

He had a deadline to meet and a position to fill and he placed a lot of faith in Tahnee Lewis. She better be worth it.

A funny knock reminiscent of the beat of an old eighties tune came from the kitchen door and he quickly saved the document he'd been working on and headed out the back.

He was big on first impressions, always had been, and the minute he opened the door he knew he was in trouble.

"Bo Bradford? I'm Tahnee Lewis, pleased to meet you."

Bo shook her hand automatically, trying not to stare at the tall, stunning blonde standing on his doorstep, and failing miserably.

He'd expected a professionally dressed woman with an equally business-like demeanour.

What he got was a denim-clad teeny bopper with challenge in her deep blue eyes and a cheeky quirk to her full lips.

This woman didn't look like the subservient type used to taking orders from a grumpy author subject to creative whims. No way.

With the face of a naughty devil and the body of an angel, she looked like one thing to him.

Trouble.

"Did I catch you at a bad time?"

Bo silently cursed his ineptitude, dropped her hand quickly and stepped aside. "No, come in. I was in the middle of a scene and I tend to get a bit distracted."

"I know exactly what you mean. I do the same thing. Once, I was so in the zone with a sketch that the toaster had a tussle with a piece of bread resulting in smoke filling the kitchen and I didn't even notice."

She smiled and his heart sank. Her face lit up with a million-dollar smile that could sell toothpaste to dentists. Combined with the sparkling blue eyes, lush mouth, and long blonde hair cut into layers that framed her heart-shaped face, Bo knew she might prove to be more of a distraction than any chapter in his current work in progress.

"Do you need a hand with any more bags?" He pointed to a small wheelie suitcase and a backpack, expecting another bag or ten in the car. The women he'd dated in the past had always needed at least five bags or cases of different sizes to house monster wardrobes. Yet another reason why he preferred living on his own.

"No, this is it."

He tried to mask his shock but must've failed by the twitching corners of her mouth.

That mouth...his gaze flicked past it, desperately trying to stay focused on her eyes. However, the harder he fought, the more tempting it became until he let his gaze dip a fraction, absorbing the shape of her lips, their fullness, their gloss.

"Bo?"

He wondered if living the life of a recluse was a good idea if he started noticing trivial things like his new illustrator's mouth. He didn't have time for dating; women were a distraction he could do without. His work was all-important and finishing this next book on time vital.

"Yeah?"

"I'd kill for a coffee," she said, sending a pointed glance at the espresso machine on the bench behind him. "If you don't mind, that is."

"No problem. How do you like it?"

For one long, loaded moment their gazes locked, her lips

parted a fraction, and he could've sworn the air sizzled with static electricity as if they'd just been through a freak storm.

How do you like it? He hadn't meant it as a come-on, far from it, and he didn't like the way she stared at him with those knowing blue eyes, as if assessing him while he grabbed two mugs out of the cupboard and all but slammed them on the granite bench top.

"I like it strong. Hot. Sweet."

Wishing she'd stop staring at him like he'd morphed into Wally's long lost brother and had sprouted ears and fur, he turned his back on her and busied himself with the coffee, hoping this wasn't a mistake. He had a relentless work ethic and a low tolerance for incompetence and though Tahnee came highly recommended, he didn't like the easy familiarity she'd already slipped into around him: her confident smile, her teasing eyes, and the unshakeable feeling she was laughing at him for being a workaholic author who didn't get out much.

"How many sugars?"

"Two, please. No milk."

He heard a rustling and crackle of paper bags being opened and he hoped she wasn't pulling out any more surprises. He'd had enough in the last few minutes to last him a while.

Moira had been the perfect co-worker: reserved, dependable, and a non-distraction with her light brown hair, no make-up and navy business suits. He'd never had the impulse to study Moira's mouth.

He'd been one hundred percent focussed on work around Moira and they'd been a cohesive team. With Tahnee, he had an awful suspicion that associating teamwork with the gorgeous blonde might lead him to ponder other creative directions altogether, directions he hadn't headed down in a long while, directions that had nothing to do with words or pictures or kids stories.

"Can I tempt you?"

Bo almost jumped out of his skin as she snuck up behind him and offered an open paper bag filled with plump croissants, the mouth-watering buttery aroma combining with a fresh, floral scent he'd inhaled earlier as she'd walked into the room.

"Thanks," he muttered, taking a croissant and turning back to pouring the coffee.

His reaction to her was insane, stupid and counter-productive. He needed Tahnee Lewis to finish his book; he didn't need her distracting him with an amused expression permanently etched on her beautiful face.

Sighing in resignation, he turned back to find her staring at him with a smug smile as if she knew exactly how annoyed he was and was enjoying every minute.

The woman was a nuisance.

The woman was a curse.

The woman had to save his butt so for now, she'd stay.

Tahnee sipped at her coffee and tried not to stare at her new boss.

Tried and failed.

Little wonder Bo Bradford didn't have a pic on his website. The number of hits he'd get would send the internet into meltdown.

She watched him fuss around the kitchen looking for a plate to dump the croissants on—Carissa's favourite almond custard croissants her sister had thrust into her hand for the two hour drive to Sydney. Tahnee hadn't felt like eating on the drive down. Lucky for her, considering Bo looked like he could do with a bit of sweetening up. He may be the hottest guy on the eastern seaboard of Australia but boy, did he need to lighten up.

"These smell good," he said, placing the plate between them and sliding into a seat opposite her as he glanced at the logo on the paper bag. "*Michelle's*? Never heard of it."

"It's a small bakery in Stockton, where I live."

Where I'll always live, she refrained from adding. She belonged in Stockton; she liked the comfort of knowing every one in town, she liked the cosy atmosphere and best of all, she'd never felt as secure as she did there, a feeling she'd do anything to preserve.

"It won't be a problem you staying here for a few weeks?"

She bit back a smile. What Mr. Nosy was really asking was if she had any ties to Stockton, namely a significant other.

Fine, her boss was entitled to know stuff like that, but with her vivid imagination—and her appreciation for a fine looking guy--she almost wished there was more than a professional interest.

Yeah, right, like her grumpy boss would be looking for a fling while trialling her for the most important job of her career. Get real.

"No problem at all. I have an overprotective sister back home who quizzed me at length about staying here, and another sister who's overseas, working in Singapore, but apart from that I'm footloose and fancy-free."

Tahnee mentally clapped a hand over her mouth. Why did she say that? Guys who looked like him would probably take it as a come-on. She needed to smarten up her act or she'd be out on her butt along with her sketchbook and charcoals.

He stared at her over the rim of his coffee mug, his steady, green gaze unwavering. "Good. We don't have time for distractions. I need to get my current book done ASAP."

"Tight deadline?"

His eyes froze, the peculiar green-blue hue the exact colour of an icy glacier she'd seen on an Alaskan documentary once. "Exactly," he said, his flat tone matching his frigid eyes. "If you've finished your coffee, I'll show you the flat."

O-kay. Was it something she said? The guy was prickly. Extremely sexy, but very prickly, and she hated having to tread on eggshells. She'd never been that type of person, preferring blunt honesty to games—which probably explained why she was eternally single and couldn't hold onto a guy beyond a few dates.

A shame, considering she wouldn't mind the whole hubby-two point five kids—white picket fence-dream one day. After all, how much more secure could she get when surrounded by a family she created?

After finishing her coffee in three quick gulps, she stood and headed for the sink to rinse her mug. "I'm ready."

Anything to diffuse the weird tension that had enveloped them; the atmosphere seemed taut since she'd arrived and when she'd asked him about his book he'd gone cold on her. Just what she needed, a temperamental artist to work with.

She turned and caught him staring at her butt before he quickly raised his gaze to eye level and she smothered a giggle. Bo blew hotter and colder than a Melbourne day. First, he froze her out, now he looked decidedly flustered. Cute, considering he had everything she valued in a guy: great pecs and flat abs hugged by a grey T-shirt, lean legs moulded by faded denim, just over six foot, amazing eyes, short back and sides, facial features arranged just right.

She was trying to play down the high cheekbones, straight nose, clean jaw and overall symmetry of his face because she needed to concentrate on work, not her boss's model potential.

"Come on, let's go. I haven't got all day," he muttered, a frown marring his brow.

This time, Tahnee couldn't stifle her smile at his barked

order and as she followed him, letting him carry her bags for being such a grump, she did a bit of butt-checking of her own, not surprised it matched the rest of his perfection.

Hmm...maybe finding inspiration for her work over the next two weeks wouldn't be so difficult after all.

Two

Wally stared at his new friend Kaz the Kangaroo. She wasn't like anyone he'd met before. She had a big smile and a great tail. But he wasn't sure if she'd be any good at helping him dig yet. All she seemed to do was talk, a lot, and he wanted to work.

Bo Bradford's blog.

"Wow, great place." Tahnee did a slow three-sixty, her smile wide.

Bo dumped her bags inside the door, glad something was going right. If she liked the flat, maybe she'd stay in it for the duration of her time here and he could drop off a draft of his work first thing every morning and leave her to it.

No distractions.

The key to his success.

"I can't wait to see where you work," she said, spinning back to face him, framed by the floor to ceiling window overlooking the pool and Sydney Harbour beyond. "Bet it's some room to keep you inspired."

So much for keeping her out of his work place and not being distracted.

"I like it. Would you like a tour now?"

"Sure." She grinned like an excited kid and he wondered if she was this carefree all the time. She seemed genuinely glad to be here, her buoyant personality grating on him.

He preferred solitude and valued peace and quiet while he worked. Moira had known that and had fitted in perfectly, while he had a nasty feeling the effervescent woman practically bouncing around like Kaz the Kangaroo, his newest creation, would drive him up the wall within the first hour.

Her light touch on his arm startled him. "Look, this is probably none of my business, but you don't seem too happy to have me here? If you've changed your mind, maybe we can figure something out? Perhaps we can work by correspondence, you email me your chapters and I'll send the sketches back, something like that?"

He glanced down at her hand, the short fingernails devoid of polish, and the bump on her third finger where she obviously rested her pencils. It was the hand of an artist, a creator, someone who would understand him, someone he could work with if he let go of the bad mood that had gripped him since she'd stepped through the back door.

He hadn't been a people person for a while now and having someone as bright and bubbly as Tahnee show up had him bristling more than he anticipated.

He forced a smile, hoping to reassure her. "I want you here. I need to get a feel for your work firsthand and emailing won't cut it for now." He shrugged. "I guess losing Moira has thrown me and I'm still trying to get my head around finding a replacement."

Her answering smile, bright, dazzling and genuine, sent remorse through him; he needed to lighten up.

"Moira was brilliant. I loved how she gave Wally those cute

expressions." She paused, nibbling on her bottom lip. "I hope I can fill her shoes."

"You don't need to fill anyone's shoes. I've seen your work. It speaks for itself, which is why you're here. Now, ready for that tour?"

"Sure," she said, though Bo glimpsed the uncertainty in her eyes, the slight droop of her mouth.

Tahnee Lewis wasn't as confident as she liked to portray.

Good. That made two of them.

———

Tahnee felt like Prue the platypus, one of Bo's creations who entered a different world each time she jumped into the creek and swam underwater.

Yeah, she felt exactly like that—amazed, wide-eyed, thrilled—as she followed Bo through his harbour-side mansion, trying not to ogle the beautiful furniture, the wide windows with stunning views of the harbour, and most of all, the guy showing her around.

This had to be an alternate reality.

Too good to be true.

"This place is amazing," she said, gaping at an exquisite painting brightening a creamy wall with its vibrant slashes of colour. "I'm not surprised you get so creative living here."

"I like it."

His simple response spoke volumes considering it was the first time he'd injected any warmth into his voice since she'd arrived.

"How long have you lived here?"

"Five years."

His short, sharp, reluctant responses implied he wasn't big on sharing personal info. No drama. She didn't need to know everything about the guy to work with him, though it would help to establish some kind of rapport. She'd keep trying. He had to crack eventually.

"You bought this place before you made it big?"

He first hit the bestseller lists four years ago, which meant he'd had a serious advance or ten before that. Or rich relatives.

He stopped suddenly and she pulled up in record time before she slammed into his back. Though copping a feel to see if those muscles felt as good as they looked beneath the cotton mightn't be so bad...

"Are you always this nosy?

"Are you always this defensive?"

He turned to face her, his body mere centimetres from hers, bringing new meaning to the phrase up close and personal. She could feel heat radiating off him, drawing her towards him like a magnet, teasing her to close the short gap between them.

"Want to see my office?"

"Is that the same as seeing your etchings?"

For a split second, she thought she'd gone too far as he stared at her in what could only be termed as shock considering his dilated pupils. Either that or he was seriously turned on and she doubted it. She would've picked up on it, but apart from staring at her butt earlier, he acted like she was an unwelcome guest rather than someone he wanted to ravish.

Just as she about to do some serious back-pedalling—or grovelling, depending how tired he'd grown of her already—he laughed, a low, husky chuckle that rippled over her like a warm summer's breeze.

"You're nothing like I expected," he said, a rueful smile transforming his face from good-looking to drop-dead gorgeous in the speed of light.

"Same here."

With no photos on social media or his website, she'd expected a bearded hermit maybe sporting the odd fang or two who howled at the moon, a bit of a freak who needed privacy to hide his many secrets. Instead, Bo was six-foot-plus of gorgeous male. And then some.

Apart from illustrating children's books, she loved to sketch beautiful things and right now her fingers itched to pick up a charcoal and transfer Bo onto paper.

His smile faded and he ran a hand over his face; she hoped it wouldn't slide his grumpy mask back in place.

"Look, I'm not a good people person. Guess I've been holed up here too long. Sorry if I came on a bit strong before."

She shrugged, wondering if surly Bo hadn't been safer than this relaxed, semi-amused Bo.

"Don't worry about it. I'm a country girl at heart and I call it how it is. My sister Carissa thinks I'm too blunt but hey, no point beating around the bush, right?"

"Right."

He smiled and it illuminated his face, taking five years off it, and had her grinning like an idiot right back at him.

Like the loaded moment back in the kitchen when they'd both stared at each other without saying a word, he stared at her now, his eyes studying her, the expression in their green depths unreadable.

"And here we have Wally's digs, where I work." He broke the spell by throwing open a door on his right and she gasped, enchanted by the room he had the audacity to call an office.

"Wow," she said, stepping into a high-ceilinged room as big as her entire flat back home, soaking up the late morning sun filtering through expansive windows, admiring yet another stunning view of the harbour and the Bridge.

She spun around slowly, eager to explore every book lining three walls on floor-to-ceiling shelves, impressed by the many book covers framed on the walls. Rich wood combined with bright rugs, natural light combined with fresh sea air drifting in an open window, and right in the middle of all this splendour stood the guy who'd hired her, looking more at home here than in the rest of the house.

"If I had a place like this to work in I'd never want to leave," she said, walking over to his desk near a window, smiling when she saw little figurines of his animal characters sitting atop his hard drive.

"I spend most of my time here."

He joined her at the desk, radiating a potent mix of heat and pheromones, the kind that called to her like nothing had before.

She really needed to get a date while she was here. Maybe she'd call up the last guy she'd had dinner with in Sydney? Pity she couldn't remember his name.

"I assume you know who these little fellas are?"

She picked up Wally, the fictional rotund wombat who'd launched his career in children's books.

"I do, but why don't you go ahead and introduce me anyway?"

"You're holding my favourite little guy in the entire world. Then this here is Prue the Platypus and Ken the Koala."

She laughed as he picked up the cute figurines no bigger than his thumb and danced them across the desk towards her, complete with formal little bows. "The prickly dude is Eddy?"

"Eddy Echidna at your service."

Eddy joined the rest of his mates on the edge of the desk and she picked him up, bringing his snout in close contact with Prue's until they were smooching.

"Hey, there's none of that stuff in my books."

"Too bad," she said, replacing Prue and Eddy in their rightful spots but with their backs to each other as if in a huff. "Now see what you've done? They've had a lovers' tiff."

He raised an eyebrow. "Maybe you should be writing the stories? Seems like you've got one hell of an imagination."

She blushed at the speculative gleam in his eyes. If he only knew exactly how vivid her imagination was. Right now it had the two of them doing what Prue and Eddy had been doing a second ago but without stopping.

If she ever had the pleasure of locking lips with sexy Bo she wouldn't stop at kissing. The few times she'd had sex in her life had been lacklustre and boring to say the least. Where were the screaming orgasms the books promised? Where were the sparks? The erogenous zones? The endless foreplay?

In her dreams, that's where.

Little wonder she stuck to meaty mysteries these days. She left the romance stuff to people who believed in magic, people like Carissa who'd been buying contemporary romances by the truckload since she hooked up with Brody.

No, romance wasn't for her. Heck, she'd settle for a feel-good fling right about now considering what was on offer...

As if. Bo was her boss and moody to boot. The last thing she needed was to bump bits with him. And by his narrow-eyed glare, he wasn't on the verge of offering her anything but her marching orders.

"Having a good imagination helps with creativity," she said, perching on the side of the desk. "You'd know all about that."

His green-eyed stare glowed emerald for a moment and she blinked, wondering if she'd imagined the speculation there, knowing it wouldn't be the first time she'd imagined a guy's interest and had been let down when she'd had a reality check.

"Sure do. Speaking of which, I hope you can kick-start your imagination ASAP."

"Uh-huh. I'm ready to hit the ground running."

"Good, because I've invented two new characters and they need to slot into this current book. Deadline's in two weeks. Think you can manage it?"

"Easy," she said, knowing it wouldn't be but up for the challenge. She needed him to offer her a permanent position so she'd sketch all night if she had to. "How do you like to work?"

In a perfect world, his answer would involve the two of them laying by the pool sipping Margaritas while brainstorming; or better yet, sprawled in the huge king-sized bed she'd glimpsed as he'd hurried her past his bedroom while giving her the grand tour.

"How about I give you a scene by scene layout and you go from there?"

"Great." She nodded. "I'm used to working like that."

"And for the new characters, I'll add a few more annotations to give you an idea of what I want."

"No probs."

Though there was one. How was she meant to concentrate if they worked in the same room?

It hadn't been a problem in the past. She'd always worked from home, enjoying the freedom of being her own boss, the freedom to work in her PJs if she wanted. She had a feeling that wouldn't go down too well around here. Not with Bo wavering between grumpy and slightly-less-than-grumpy depending on his mood.

"You can work in here if you like," he said begrudgingly, like he preferred she wouldn't.

Which of course sparked her snarky nature and ensured she would. "You sure I won't get in your way? I can work anywhere."

"Here is fine," he said, sounding less than enthused. "That way, we can get a feel for how each other works, iron out any kinks in the early stages before they become a problem."

"Okay. When do we start?"

He glanced at his watch, an expensive silver designer number that probably cost more than her rent for a year.

"How about after lunch?"

"Sounds good."

She waited, unsure whether he expected her to join him or whether he'd relegated her to back-door status again.

"You're welcome to join me."

By his flat monotone, she'd be as welcome as a snake at a picnic.

"Thanks, but I'll get settled in and grab something later. Meet you back here at one?"

He nodded and turned back to his desk, effectively dismissing her.

Tahnee shook her head and headed for the flat. Maybe working with the sexy author wouldn't be a problem after all. If she focussed on his moodiness that wavered back and forth at whim, concentrating on work instead of his great bod and handsome face would be a cinch.

Three

"Wally scratched his belly, sat back, and watched Kaz flick her long tail from side to side. He reckoned she was doing it on purpose, to distract him. It was working. With an annoyed growl, he turned away and starting digging harder, his claws making little headway in the dirt. Beyond frustrating."

Bo Bradford's blog.

"Meet my latest buddies. Kaz the Kangaroo and Keely the Kookaburra."

Bo opened the top drawer of his desk and pulled out the cutest imitation kangaroo and kookaburra Tahnee had ever seen.

"They're adorable."

"They will be if you draw them right," he said, plonking them into her outstretched hands. "Kaz is Wally's new mate, his latest best friend, and I have a feeling Wally's developing a little crush on her. Keely is the joker of the pack. She eggs everyone on and spends all day laughing at them."

"I love it," she said, wondering how such a serious guy could have such a vivid imagination—and wondering if it extended to other facets of his life. "The kids are going to love it too."

"That's what counts." He handed her several cardboard flatlays where he'd pasted bits of paper.

"Here are the first three scenes I need illustrated. In the first one, I need Wally to look wary as he meets Kaz while she's sassy and overconfident. In the second, Kaz is showing off and Wally's doing his best to look bored while Keely laughs her head off. In the third, Wally's sneaking bashful peeks at Kaz who loves the attention. Is that enough info?"

"You'll see soon enough," she said, taking the layouts and heading to the huge royal blue suede couch in the corner, her fingers itching to get started.

"There's a smaller desk over there if you need it. Moira used to work there."

It figured. Tahnee glanced at the neat as a pin, generic grey desk with its PC, in-tray and standard office chair, and plopped onto the comfy couch.

"I'll be fine over here. I prefer to be comfortable when I work."

"Suit yourself." He shrugged and turned away but not before she'd seen his bemused expression.

So she confused him? What was new? She confused most guys she came into contact with. They didn't understand her 'honesty is best' policy, especially when applied to their inadequacies. And she told them. Life was too short to waste mucking about when she hoped to find the right guy eventually. Not that she was holding her breath.

Tahnee settled into the cushions, sighing with pleasure as they moulded around her. Now this was a couch she could work on. Her own at home felt similar: supportive yet comfortable, firm yet squishy, just right.

"Are you okay?"

She looked up to find Bo staring at her with more of that confusion she'd come to expect.

"Fine, just getting comfortable."

"Right," he said, the corners of his mouth twitching as he ducked behind his computer screen.

"You wouldn't understand," she muttered, casting surreptitious glances at his state of the art desk with its sleek lines, huge glass top, orderly stacked trays, and built-in pen holder. His straight-backed ergonomic chair finished the ensemble.

She couldn't work like that, all neat and uptight. In the later stages, when she had to present the final product to the publisher, sure, but now, in the early free-for-all brainstorming stage? No way.

After setting Kaz and Keely on the seat next to her, she rummaged in her bag for sketchpad and charcoals. She'd brought half her workspace with her, much to Carissa's disgust. Her sister had insisted she take more changes of wardrobe while she'd rather have a larger choice of charcoals than shoes.

Besides, as she'd suspected, Bo didn't look the dress up and entertain type. A guy who kept to himself, valued his privacy enough to keep his pic offline, and practically snapped at her rather than holding a civilised conversation, probably didn't throw huge parties, so the several pairs of jeans she'd packed would do just fine.

"Why don't you have a photo on your website or social media profiles?" She'd wanted to know and now seemed as good a time as any to ask considering the thought had popped into her head.

"Not relevant to the type of books I sell. Kids don't want to see me, they want to know when the next instalment of Wally and Co. is coming out."

He didn't raise his head from behind the screen and she

hated that. Doris, her foster mum, had taught her to always look someone in the eye, especially when they were talking to you. Well, if Mr. Personality didn't have any manners, she'd prod him until he reacted.

"But isn't your website a major promotional tool alongside social media? Wouldn't other professionals in the industry want to know about the man behind the phenomenon?"

"I let my work do the talking."

Another brush-off. Time to get tough. "Do you wear a disguise to book signings too? You know, to let your *work* do the talking."

That grabbed his attention as he poked his head around the screen, exasperation warring with annoyance if his frown and thinned lips were any indication.

"I go dressed as Wally. Now, can I get back to work?"

"You're kidding, right?"

Either the guy had a serious personality disorder preventing him from letting the world see him for who he was or he was hiding something. She'd bet a year's worth of almond custard croissants it was the latter.

"I value my privacy and the kids love it. End of story."

"That's what you think," she said, as he ducked behind the screen again, muttering something she couldn't hear. "You're serious, aren't you?"

"Uh-huh," he said, the brittle edge to his voice signalling he was fast running out of patience.

Too bad. She liked knowing who she worked with. It gave her a better feel for the characters and ultimately, produced a better end result.

"You're not a criminal on the run?"

"No."

"Are you agoraphobic?"

"No."

At least he was responding even if he wouldn't look at her. She took it as a sign of encouragement.

"I know. You've got a bunny boiler after you."

At last, some attention as his head snapped up from behind the screen. "A what?"

"The type of woman who becomes obsessed with the guy she fancies. You know, like in that movie where the scorned mistress goes into the guy's home and puts his rabbit on the stove and—"

"I get the picture." He held up both hands as if trying to ward her off. Like that was going to work. "Don't you ever shut up?"

"Only when I get the truth," she said, twirling a charcoal nub between her thumb and forefinger like a baton. "If we're going to work together, I need to know what makes Bo Bradford tick. I need to know what inspires you, what gives you the creative edge over the competition, basically who you are. That way, I can get a real feel for your work and produce the kind of pictures you want."

"That's a crock." He stood, folded his arms in classic defensive posture, and glared at her. "Moira worked with me for years and didn't pry half as much as you."

"*Moira, Moira, Moira.*" She put on her best little girl's voice though she stopped short of poking her tongue out at him. "In case you haven't noticed, I'm not Moira. And by the look of that prim and proper desk, I'll never be anything like Moira, so get over it. I'm here to work with the best and that's what I intend to produce for you too. If you *work* with me, as in two people giving and taking. Think you can do that?"

His eyes narrowed to green slits, shooting enough disapproval to scorch her to cinders on the spot. "You do realise I can fire you right now?"

A tide of panic washed over her but she ignored it. She had a feeling bossy Bo was all bark and no bite. "I don't think you want to do that, what with your deadline in two weeks and these new characters to incorporate and my outstanding reputation and—"

"Just get on with it."

He sat and hid behind his screen again, but not before she'd seen his worried expression.

For a guy who faced deadlines all the time he was acting mighty strange about this one, almost as if it were life and death. Another Bo Bradford mystery to solve...goody.

With an extra loud exasperated sigh—to tell Bo he may have won the battle but the war was only beginning—she tucked her feet under her, rested her sketchbook on her lap and studied Keely's pointy beak.

Bo had secrets, plenty of them by his ridiculous reaction to her questions, and if there was one thing she liked more than illustrating it was solving mysteries. Unfortunately for him, she was darn good at it too.

Let him give her the brush-off and go all recalcitrant on her.

She'd find out what was biting his butt eventually.

―――

It took a superhuman effort for Bo to concentrate on the screen and fill it with words. Whether those words actually made sense or not was another matter but right now it took all his willpower to write and not cross his office to throttle Tahnee.

He knew she'd be trouble the first second he laid eyes on her but he had no idea how much. She was inquisitive, pushy, brash, and way too confident for her own good. And she had an annoying habit of nibbling her bottom lip while she concentrated which drove him to distraction.

"How's it coming along?"

He frowned and stood, needing to stretch, needing to do something other than snap at her for distracting him with her inane chatter for the umpteenth time in the last hour.

"Okay. I've managed four pages," *of crap*. "How about you? Can I take a look?"

"Sure."

She stretched, linking her hands and reaching overhead, pulling her T shirt tight over her breasts and exposing a band of flat, tanned midriff. Great. She was disruptive enough without him noticing her impressive physical attributes.

"Here, come and take a look."

She picked up several bits of paper and patted the seat next to her, leaving him no option but to sit, when the last thing he needed in his current aggravated state was to waste more time noticing her when he'd rather be working.

"Well?"

He rifled through the pictures, admiration mingling with relief. She was good. Very good. Better than Moira and that was saying something, considering Moira had worked with the best in England before spending the last four years with him.

"Aren't you going to say something? I'm having a minor conniption over here."

He looked at her, surprised to see genuine concern. "You might not be anything like Moira but you're sure sounding like her. Conniption is definitely a Moira word."

She waved her hand in his face as if trying to erase his words. "Never mind all that. Tell me what you think of the illustrations."

He reached out to reassure her without thinking, laying a hand on her arm, the kind of impersonal yet reassuring touch he'd give to anybody. But Tahnee wasn't anybody. She was a vibrant, stunning, young woman and she had him more distracted than he'd been in years.

He dropped his hand quickly. "They're great. I'm very impressed."

"Really?"

The hope he glimpsed in her eyes had him feeling like an ogre. Perhaps he had been a bit tough on her earlier? After all, she had a point about the whole 'getting to know each other to work better' thing.

"Really. Now, how about dinner? I'm cooking." No big deal. He cooked for himself every night.

"But it's still early..." she trailed off, glancing out the window at the growing dusk and looking back at him in surprise. "We must've been at it for a while."

"Four hours, give or take an hour."

"Wow."

She flipped her sketchbook shut and slid the charcoal into a box, a strange expression flitting across her face.

"Is something wrong?"

She shook her head. "I guess I thought it would take me a while to get comfortable here. You know, get into the swing of things. I'm pretty fast when I get into the zone back home but never expected it to happen so quickly here."

He knew exactly what she meant and for a brief second it felt good to be on the same wavelength. Working with Moira had been different: she'd taken his scenes, turned her back on him for the day and barely spoken, often sliding the completed work into his in-tray the next morning if she took it home.

Tahnee created the same way he did. She understood the thrill of losing yourself in your work, when time became irrelevant and hours passed in what felt like mere minutes. He loved being in the zone and it looked like he'd met his match. Figuratively speaking, of course.

"I'm glad you're comfortable here," he said, handing back her sketches. "And I'm even gladder you can produce that quality of work so quickly. You're very talented."

"That's what they all say." She sent him a coy glance from beneath her lashes, smiling broadly when he shuffled like a rabbit ready to bolt.

"Let me guess. Moira didn't flirt with you either."

"Hell no."

The thought of forty-five year old Moira with her short bob, wire-rimmed specs, navy business suits and no-nonsense shoes flirting with him seemed as incongruous as him heading back to the world of finance to earn a living.

Not a chance.

Tahnee laughed and stood in one, fluid movement, her lithe body showing little sign of being cramped in one position for so long.

"Well, if I get out of hand, you know what you have to do."

"What's that?"

"Spank me."

While he struggled with deciphering whether she was kidding or not, she sashayed out the door, leaving him torn between wanting to sack her on the spot or holing up in his room until she left him in peace at the end of the fortnight.

"This fettuccine carbonara is sensational," Tahnee said, twirling a long length of pasta around her fork and mopping up the thick, creamy sauce with it. "Where did you learn to cook like this?"

Bo raised his wine glass and for a second, she thought he wouldn't answer. Damn the man and his secrets.

"I spent six months in Italy a while back. I got hooked then."

"That must've been exciting," she said, forking pasta into her mouth and sighing in contentment.

She loved food, and courtesy of a fast metabolism and her height, she could indulge her passion on a regular basis. However, her culinary masterpieces consisted of roast lamb and veggies, followed by a fresh fruit pavlova. Not exactly world class cuisine.

"Yeah, Italy was amazing. My brother and I toured the whole country." His lips compressed as if he'd said too much.

"You have a brother?"

She laid down her fork and reached for a chunk of bread to mop up the little sauce remaining in her bowl, trying to keep her question casual when in fact she was dying to get an insight into this enigmatic guy.

"Yeah."

"And?"

Would this guy ever give her more than the barest of polite answers? She'd known he was a recluse but he could use a year's worth of social etiquette classes.

He sipped at his shiraz, staring into the wine before he finally laid down his glass.

"We're not that close."

"Bad case of sibling rivalry, huh?"

"Nothing that interesting. We're just different people now."

"You must've been close at one point to travel to Italy together?"

He glowered at her, his green eyes flinty. "Don't you ever get tired of prying into other people's business?"

"No," she said, sending him a wry smile while wondering how far she could push him.

This was interesting stuff. Much better than eating in silence with the occasional polite 'pass the Parmesan please' or 'more garlic bread' thrown in.

With an exasperated sigh, he leaned back in his chair and folded his arms.

"We used to work together in our dad's financial company, one of the biggest in Australia. Brennan and I were good buddies but we don't dig the same things anymore. He's into making money at any cost and living the high life, I've finally followed my dream and done the creative thing. He's Dad's golden boy and I'm fine with that, though we just don't see eye to eye these days. My father respects my need for solitude but Brennan doesn't get it. He can't understand how I like to be hidden away here writing rather than out drinking and partying."

She stared at Bo in surprise, more by him speaking more than two words to her rather than the information he'd imparted.

"You were in finance before you were published? That's a big career change."

For the first time since she arrived, he smiled, a fully fledged grin that set her pulse thundering in response. The guy was seriously gorgeous when he wasn't being the silent-tyrant boss or hiding behind his grumpy mask.

"Yeah, a huge change. I can actually use my brain for manipulating animal figures rather than tossing around financial figures. It's great."

Encouraged by his smile—and the fact he hadn't bitten her head off for asking so many probing questions—she said, "So what prompted you to make the change?"

"Kay." His smile faded and he took a sip of wine.

For some strange reason, hearing him say a woman's name woke a little green-eyed monster Tahnee never knew existed. To make matters worse, the annoying monster clawed out, sending a sharp stab of jealousy through her.

Dousing the monster with a good dumping of common sense, she said, "Kay?"

"Ex-girlfriend. We met through work, hung out a lot, thought hooking up would be a good move but we were too different. She pointed out I was more wrapped up in the jottings I made in a notebook I carried around with me than her and she was right. There were no hard feelings. In fact, I was relieved when she dumped me to take off with our managing director, even more grateful when I realised she'd given me a long overdue wake-up call. I took those jottings, drafted my first book, got an agent and the rest...well, you probably know the rest, a snoop like you."

His words didn't bear any malice and she grinned at him, the green-eyed monster picking up some pom-poms and doing a happy dance. The woman sounded like a mercenary cow and from where Tahnee sat—opposite an intelligent, creative, gorgeous guy—it was Kay's loss.

"More wine?"

"No thanks." Her head already had a fuzzy tinge, and combined with feeling sorry for her jilted boss, the cosy ambience of the kitchen, and the slight crush she'd developed on Bo in less than twenty-four hours, the last thing she needed was more alcohol. "Though can I ask a question?"

"Haven't you asked enough?" He spoke without rancour, his eyes defrosting to a warmer green.

"You said your family's finance company is big? I've never heard of the Bradfords."

"Bradford is a pseudonym."

"Oh."

Obvious, considering his obsession with privacy. "Then I guess it's no use me asking what your real name is?"

He topped up his wine glass, a small smile playing around his mouth as he ignored her.

"Come on, Bo, you know I'm naturally curious." She put on her best wheedling voice and his smile turned to outright laughter.

"You're naturally *nosy* and you said one question."

"Give me your real name and I promise I'll stop." She held

up two fingers to her forehead in a salute. At least, that's what she hoped it looked like. Otherwise, he might interpret it as a very rude sign.

"Bogart."

She leaned forward, not sure if she'd heard correctly. "Pardon?"

"My real name is Bogart."

"Your first name, you mean?"

He nodded. "Mum had a thing for Casablanca."

"No kidding." She fiddled with the stem of her empty wine glass, wondering if she could push him just a tad further. "So it's Bogart…?"

"That's your quota of questions for today, Ms. Nosy. Now, would you like a coffee?"

He stood and headed for the sink, the conversation closed.

Not that she could blame him. She'd been pushing him all day and for someone she could've sworn didn't want her here, he'd taken it in his stride. She valued blunt honesty and fostered an intense curiosity for mysteries; that didn't mean everyone else did. Overall, he'd been a good sport and she really needed to give the guy a break.

With that in mind, she stood, dumped her bowl in the sink, and said, "You wash, I'll dry, okay?"

"Fine."

Though her decision to tone down her personality and be nice didn't last long as she saw his solemn mask slide back into place. Picking up a dish-cloth from the oven handle, she eyed his tempting butt and flicked it with the cloth ever-so-lightly.

"What the hell?" He swivelled so fast, water and soap suds flew everywhere and she squealed, swatting away flying bubbles and water droplets, creating a diversion.

He didn't buy it.

"Did you just flick my butt?"

She struggled to keep a straight face, she really did, but fighting losing battles wasn't one of her strong points.

"When I pulled the dish-cloth off the rack, it might've skimmed you. Accidentally, of course," she added, knowing her burgeoning grin wouldn't convince him.

It didn't.

"I guess I should be grateful it wasn't your hands," he said, a glimmer of a smile working its way through his grim expression.

"Believe me, you'll know if my hands ever find their way there," she said, turning away with sudden embarrassment and heading for the table, trying to appear busy clearing it.

What had she been thinking? That's the last time she'd drink around him. No telling what she might do considering she couldn't get the image of her hands on his butt out of her head now she'd thought about it.

"Tahnee?"

"Yeah?"

She didn't look up from the table, gathering the salt and pepper shakers, the olive oil bottle, and the parmesan cheese, rearranging them like a general organising field placements for his troops and wishing the floor would open up and swallow her.

"You're an inquisitive woman and I bet you know a lot about me, such as the fact I value my privacy and have lived like a recluse for the last five years?"

"Yeah?"

She continued to fiddle with the cutlery, intense embarrassment at what she'd just done seeping through her body until she wanted to bolt from the kitchen—and the house—and never come back.

"I haven't dated much in that time."

"So?" She kept her answer non-committal, wishing the

sandstone tiled floor would crack open and swallow her whole.

"Well, you shouldn't push a guy like that."

"I don't know what came over me," she said, feeling like the worst kind of fool and hoping this didn't ruin her chances of securing long-term work with him.

She sensed him come up behind her a second too late as his hands settled on her waist and turned her around so her startled gaze met his serious stare.

"Good. In that case, you'll understand I don't know what's come over me too," he said, a split second before his lips locked on hers.

Four

Wally and Kaz finished dinner, then stretched out by the camp fire. They drank mugs of hot billy tea and told stories. But Wally couldn't concentrate. Kaz kept smiling at him and he didn't like it. It confused him. He went to bed but when he said goodnight to Kaz, she blew him a kiss. He waddled away, his tummy feeling funny.

Bo Bradford's blog.

Tahnee had never been kissed like this before.

She'd had the perfunctory goodnight kiss, the sweet-but-no-spark kiss, the pseudo-passionate kiss, and the comfortable-as-old-socks kiss.

But never in her twenty five years had she had this kind of impulsive, opportunistic, toe-curling, clash of lips that ignited every latent hormone in her body.

She came alight; there was no other way to describe it as Bo's lips coaxed hers with a steady, sensual assault. He didn't have to do much coaxing as she opened her mouth, wanting him to taste her, to tease her, to kiss her like she'd never been kissed before.

He deepened the kiss, sucking her bottom lip, nibbling it, flicking his tongue along it as her body melted against him in a hot heap of mushy bones and muscles. Every inch of her skin craved his touch with an intensity that left her breathless as she slid her hands under the hem of his T-shirt and encountered firm, warm skin covering hard muscle.

A low groan rumbled in the back of his throat, a sexy sound prompting her to slide her hands ever so slowly downwards, toying with the waistband of his jeans.

He broke the kiss, staring at her like she'd lost her mind. Not fair, considering he'd been the one to start it. But she had the roving hands. Yeah, well, she couldn't help it if she was a tactile person. It came with the creativity gene.

He's creative too...which had her fingers itching to explore him all over again.

"That's some goodnight kiss," she said, slipping out of his embrace and thrusting her hands in her jean pockets as if sharing sizzling kisses with her boss was par for the course.

"That never should've happened," he snapped, running a hand through his hair.

She forced a fake smile. "Hey, don't beat yourself up over it. Us creative types have a lot of crazy impulses. It's no big deal."

Tell that to her heart that had kick-started the minute his mouth locked on hers and hadn't slowed down since.

"I don't do impulsive. And I sure as hell don't go around kissing women I barely know." His lips compressed in a thin, hard line and she wondered how he could stand there and act so damn self-righteous when all she wanted to do was jump him and pick up where they'd left off.

She shrugged, eyeing the doorway. Time to make a hasty exit while she still had some dignity left. Glossing over the kiss was one thing, reliving it in detail—with her kissing him again —another.

"Like I said, it's no biggie. I'm cute, you couldn't help yourself. These things happen."

"No, they don't. Not to me. I'm sorry."

He glared at her as if this was all her fault; technically true considering she'd flicked him first. But she'd only wanted to help him loosen up a bit, to lose the uptight attitude and the grim face, not kiss her silly.

Maybe it was the wine, maybe it was a stomach full of pasta, or maybe it was the kiss to end all kisses, but she could've hung around the kitchen all night staring down the angry guy who looked like he wanted to strangle her rather than kiss her again.

"We need to call it a night," he said, bracing his arms against the bench top and leaning backwards, highlighting a great set of biceps and a chest she'd almost had the pleasure of exploring in greater detail.

"I guess we should."

She didn't move. Her mind transmitted the message to her legs but it got lost in the translation considering it had to bypass her lower regions throbbing with want.

Seconds passed, maybe minutes, she had no idea, as they stood there, gazes locked, fury and fire in his, challenge and uncertainty in hers.

She'd never been kissed like that before, and by her boss, no less. And just like that, the message finally transmitted to her legs and she took a step back. "See you in the morning. What time do you want to start?"

"I'm an early riser. How does nine suit you?"

"Fine, but that's not early."

"I would've had a swim and put in two hours by then."

She grimaced. She'd never been a morning person. "Nine is fine."

It wasn't the thought of getting up early that was the problem as much as the thought of spending another thirteen days in his company that had her on tenterhooks.

"Good. See you then."

"Right."

He hadn't moved, his casual pose showing off the body that had tempted her to lose it a few minutes ago—long legs, broad shoulders, great arms—and she briefly wondered if he was doing it on purpose. Sort of like showing her what she was missing out on.

Too bad. She wasn't the one who'd come to their senses first and ended that kiss. Though she should have been.

She made it to the door before he spoke.

"That kiss was a big mistake and will never happen again."

"Never is a long time," she said, tossing him a teasing smile over her shoulder before walking out the door.

Bo paced his office.

He'd tried booting up his computer and working: nothing.

He'd tried reading the latest sci-fi release from his favourite author: he'd read the same paragraph six times.

He'd even tried rolling the weird metal stress balls Moira had given him as a going away present in the palm of his hand: he'd almost ended up flinging them against the wall.

Nothing alleviated his frustration or his anger.

He'd kissed Tahnee.

A stupid, spur of the moment impulse that even now, he couldn't believe he'd given into. He prided himself on being in control and his ability to focus on the task at hand, and right now that meant finishing the book that would catapult his career into the stratosphere.

It had to be the close proximity. He'd been holed up in here for the last few months working fourteen hour days trying to fulfil his latest contract, all with the aim to make it big in the competitive overseas market. Though in reality he'd locked himself away for the last five years, focussed on swapping one life for another. While his work may be blossoming, the seclusion had addled his brains, resulting in him jumping the first attractive woman to come near him in years.

He was lucky she was so understanding. Then again, he probably wouldn't have kissed her if she hadn't flicked him with the dishcloth. A bold, sassy move, the kind of unpredictability he found so appealing considering it was the complete antithesis of him, a boring stiff who buried himself in work.

He stopped pacing, sat on the couch and picked up the sketches Tahnee had completed that afternoon, flicking through them and not surprised to find himself smiling by the end. She'd captured Kaz perfectly with a cheeky grin, huge, doe-like eyes and long eyelashes, giving the kangaroo an innocent yet teasing glint. Poor Wally didn't stand a chance.

Just like him if he didn't get his ass into gear and get this book done without further complications. For that's all the kiss was in reality, an unwanted complication, a lapse in judgement, a blip on the radar.

Apart from craving complete quiet while he worked, he'd stopped socialising for a reason. Relationships were complicated and distracting and every woman he'd ever been involved with had expected more than he was willing to give. After Kay, he'd tried to keep dating casual but some women didn't do casual very well, they always wanted more. Whereas his characters liked him just he way he was.

A kiss could lead to expectations on Tahnee's part and it annoyed the hell out of him he'd slipped up like that. Come tomorrow, he'd be all business again and put his stupid, momentary lapse out of his mind.

For now, he'd update his blog; anything to get his brain concentrating on getting words from his fingertips to the screen and not on the fact a gorgeous woman lay in bed, probably in something suitably skimpy, less than twenty metres away.

His fingers clattered on the keyboard, his eyes glued to the screen, but his mind refused to come to the party and he logged off within five minutes, heading to bed in a frustrated huff.

———

Tahnee sat cross-legged on her bed and picked up her cell, flipping it over and over. She could ring Carissa but then she'd be likely to blurt out what had happened with Bo in the kitchen earlier tonight and she couldn't comprehend it yet let alone articulate it.

Maybe she'd send a text instead, something along the lines of SOS?

Ever since Brody had bought Carissa a new fancy smartphone for her birthday, her sister had been texting madly, preferring to text rather than chat. However, trying to type a message to describe her bizarre day would take far too long. Besides, what could she say?

That her boss was a moody grouch who looked ready to fire her for asking too many questions?

That he was an uptight hermit who needed to loosen up a little? Or a lot as the case may be.

That she'd provoked him into kissing her when she could see it was the last thing he'd wanted to do?

She'd seen it the minute he broke the kiss, anger flaring in his eyes, his lips settling into their residual thin line. She'd been tempted to bait him further but his grim expression combined with his frigid apology had reinforced she'd pushed him enough for one day.

After all, she needed this job more than anything.

So her boss was intriguing, talented, sexy, and kissed like a dream? She needed to forget the minor aberration of the kitchen kiss and focus on work and convincing him he couldn't live without her for his bestselling books.

But damn it, she couldn't get him out of her head.

She'd taken a long, hot bath in lavender crystals to relax after making it back to the flat; it hadn't worked.

She'd tried reading a few pages of the best mystery novel ever; it hadn't worked.

She'd tried meditating, which she did on the odd occasion to unwind; it hadn't worked.

In fact, the meditation had been the worst as every time she tried to visualise a quiet, peaceful spot, Bo would pop into her mind and she'd remember how he'd tasted—warm and fruity from the wine—and how he'd held her—nice and tight and pressed up against all those firm muscles—and her relaxation was shot.

The more she tried meditating, the hotter and more worked up she became. She really needed a date soon if she had designs on her dour boss.

Biting her lower lip, her thumb slid across the keypad, torn between wanting to give Carissa a little gossip or a lot. Her sister didn't possess half the insatiable curiosity she did, always poking her nose into other people's business as Bo had been too eager to point out.

She couldn't help it. Maybe it was a genetic thing? She'd never find out now and for the first time in ages, the hot sting of tears burned her eyes as she wished her mum or Doris were here. She barely remembered her mum other than the great cuddles she used to give, smelling of toasted cinnamon, but

Doris had been good to chat things over with, always ready with a pragmatic word or objective viewpoint.

She could certainly do with some objectivity now. She needed someone to tell her 'yeah, your boss is attractive but so what?' She needed to hear 'so he kissed you, big deal, move on, get a life.' Most of all, she needed to hear 'if you botch this job, you'll lose your dream.'

Sighing, she popped the cell in her bedside drawer and slipped beneath the cotton covers, not ready for Carissa's inquisition if she texted her. Not that she'd get much sleep. She hadn't been this wound up in a long time. The guys she dated in the past had been interesting enough but none had lit her fire like that one unexpected kiss from Bo. A totally alien concept considering she preferred to get to know a guy first and the attraction tended to grow from there.

She'd never had an instant wham-bam, in-your-face, sexual attraction before and it had her tied in knots. Usually lighthearted and flirty with guys, she couldn't do that anymore with Bo courtesy of their kiss; he might misconstrue the slightest bit of teasing and where would they end up then?

Her eyes squeezed shut to block out the image of the two of them in bed, only to snap open a second later when the erotic pictures filtering across her mind intensified. She never did this. Picturing herself having sex with a guy she'd only just met, not to mention lusting after a work colleague.

It was crazy.

It was dangerous.

Worst of all, it left her with an incredible lust for a guy who should be off-limits.

Work was the answer. If she stayed focussed on getting the job done right, her irrational instant crush on Bo would fade into the background. They could pretend like the heavenly kiss never happened.

She could do this.

No more dish-cloth flicking, no more ogling his butt—or biceps or pecs or abs—and keep flirting to a minimum. Concentrate on sketching Wally, Kaz and crew, dazzle Bo with her illustrating skills, and keep her mind on the job.

Snuggling into bed, she turned onto her side and closed her eyes. Now she had a definite plan of action she could face whatever bossy Bo had to dish out.

Starting first thing in the morning, she'd show him her new ultra professional side.

She could do this.

Now, if only she could forget the way he kissed...

Five

Wally had a lot of work to do. He'd fallen behind thanks to Kaz and her constant chatter. He was grumpier than usual and now he'd been invited to some stupid party down by the waterhole. What was worse, he'd probably have to invite her just to be nice. Why him?

Bo Bradford's blog.

"Damn this to hell."

Tahnee looked up from her sketchpad and the drawings she'd been focussed for the last few hours, determinedly not looking Bo's way.

Wombat with a sore head wouldn't come close to describing how grumpy he'd been this morning. He'd barely spoken to her, banging away at his keyboard like a man possessed and replying to her questions regarding work in short, snapped syllables. She should be grateful. If this is how he reacted after one kiss, she'd hate to see if he really lost his head and went wild.

"What's up?"

He ignored her for a moment and she considered flinging one of her sketch-pads at him. He really was the most rude, gloomy, insufferable man she'd ever met and for the life of her she couldn't understand how she could find him remotely attractive.

Though he did have a great body and a sensational smile... on the too few occasions she'd seen it so far.

Slumping back in his chair, he locked his hands behind his head and sent her an exasperated stare. "I forgot about this boring publishing awards thing on tonight. My agent just sent me an email and said I have to go."

"And that's a problem because?"

Though she already knew the answer. Mr. Reclusive took himself way too seriously and if he treated her like a constant interruption he had to endure, she could only imagine what he'd be like socialising at a fancy function.

"I don't have time for it."

She could've agreed with him and gone back to her drawing, but where was the fun in that?

"Perhaps you should make time. Being an author isn't just about creating, it's about marketing and promotion and putting yourself out there. And I'd hazard a guess if your agent says it's important, it is?"

His eyes narrowed to green slits, his almost permanent frown in place. "Do you bother with all that mundane stuff? *Putting yourself out there?*"

She shook her head, wishing he could leave for his night out now and leave her in peace for the rest of the day. She'd get a heck of a lot more work done that way without his brooding presence distracting her.

"I'm not an author. No one's interested in schmoozing with the illustrator, they want the person who links the words into magical sentences and makes a bucket-load of moola, not some artist who gets a kick out of drawing funky little pictures for kids."

He didn't respond, staring at her like she'd recited one of his prize-winning books from memory. His intense stare didn't waver and he leaned forward, making her squirm under his scrutiny.

"You're wrong."

"About what?"

He hit print on his keyboard, crossed to the printer and grabbed a sheet of paper before walking over to the couch and handing her a copy of an email.

"People in the industry are interested in the illustrators. I'm surprised you haven't been to one of these bashes before."

"Not interested."

She waved away the email, trying to act like she got invited to posh publishing events every day when she'd only ever been invited to one but had come down with gastro at the last minute and couldn't go. Not that she'd minded. She had a feeling dressed-up denim wouldn't fit the dress code anyway.

He sat next to her and all but slapped the email on her sketchpad. "I'm not interested either but if I have to go, you do too."

"No, I don't." She didn't glance at the invitation, preferring to glare at him instead.

"This is a business event. While you're working for me, I expect you to act like a professional and that includes accompanying me to this."

He jabbed at the email on her pad, the paper making sharp, crinkling noises, the same type of noise it would make when she screwed it up into a ball and lobbed it in the trash.

"No."

Where did he get off telling her to act professional when he was the one who'd kissed her last night?

So much for trying to forget that incident and concentrate

on work. It wouldn't work to her advantage if she flung it in his face now but boy, was she tempted.

"You'll find all the details here including the dress code." He spoke as if he hadn't heard her refusal, his gaze flicking over her faded denim hipsters and "I RULE" pink T-shirt. "And if you don't have anything suitable to wear, you can have two hours off this afternoon to go shopping."

"You're crazy." She stood and stalked to the window, needing to put some distance between them before she did something silly, like shove his invitation up his expensive cashmere cable-knit.

"Not yet, but I will be if you continue carrying on like this."

His voice had risen and she whirled to face him, ready to give him a piece of her mind, when he held up his hands in surrender.

"Look, I know this evening will be boring but I thought it might be a great opportunity for you to meet some industry heavyweights. Get to know some people. It can only help your career long term, whatever happens at the end of our two weeks working together. What do you think?"

She thought it sucked. Not his invitation or his thoughtfulness in thinking of her career, but the fact she'd leapt to all sorts of silly conclusions when he first asked, the main one being he was asking her out on a date.

Injecting enthusiasm into her voice, she said, "Okay, you've convinced me with all your perfectly logical, rational arguments. I'll go. Thanks for asking."

"No problems."

He turned away and returned to his desk and she headed back to the couch, picking up the invitation that had slithered to the floor. "How formal is this cocktail dress code?"

He sat behind his desk, the tiny crease between his brows

deepening as he pondered her question. "The girls don't wear long dresses, just those mid-calf thingies?"

She sent him a rueful grin. "Thanks for the fashion tip. I'll make sure I grab an appropriate thingy later on this afternoon."

His mouth twitched and she wished he'd laugh for once, a genuine, roaring outburst or even a subdued chuckle. If he was this sociable tonight, she was in for a real treat. Not.

"We'll leave at eight," he said, effectively dismissing her as he returned to clattering on his keyboard and she resisted the urge to flip him the finger.

So her boss only saw her as an unknown nobody who needed an introduction into the big, bad world of publishing?

She'd show him.

Several hours later, Tahnee was ready to give up. Even chatting to Carissa for fifteen minutes on the phone while she shopped hadn't calmed her and she was ready to find a big, black garbage bag, tear neck and arm holes in it, and see how Mr. Grumpy liked that outfit better than her jeans.

How could finding one dress be this difficult? With a plethora of boutiques to choose from, she'd managed to bypass every single one: too pretentious, too expensive, too daggy.

She trudged up the main street of Rose Bay, feet dragging, wishing she had genie powers and could blink the perfect dress into her wardrobe, when she saw it. A tiny vintage clothing shop tucked between a vegan café and a day spa. However, the shop hadn't grabbed her attention as much as the dress in the window; a stunning ice-blue halter neck dress with a cinched waist and flaring, pleated skirt.

In that split second, a confirmed jeans girl fell in love... with a dress.

Hurrying into the shop in case the dress vanished like a figment of her imagination—or worse, into some uppity woman's manicured hands—she pounced on the bewildered shop assistant, made frantic hand signals toward the dress and had whipped off her clothes in the dressing room in under a minute.

It probably wouldn't fit. It would probably make her hips look huge and her tummy bulge. But then she zipped into it and...as Tahnee stared at herself in the mirror, she couldn't help but grin. Perfection. She'd never owned anything like it. The dress had to possess magical qualities because no way did she look this good. And the colour...it made her eyes sparkle and her skin glow and made her feel a million dollars.

Sighing, she reached for the price tag, aware vintage shops weren't usually expensive but this was Rose Bay, a ritzy suburb renowned for extravagance. Squeezing her eyes shut and peeking at the tag through a half squint, she saw two zeros and her heart sank. No way would she spend hundreds of dollars on a dress she'd probably only wear once. However, as she opened her other eye, her heart danced for there was a measly little one in front of the zeros.

For a hundred bucks, the dress was a steal and she shimmied out of it, hung it on the peg, and pulled her jeans and top back on. She loved denim but apparently satin was in a league of its own.

She almost skipped to the cashier counter. "I'll take it," she said, thrusting her money at the young shop assistant who stared at her with fear. The poor girl probably didn't see too many demented women in hipsters barging into the shop on a mission.

Once the dress had been wrapped in tissue paper and bagged, Tahnee sent a glorious smile the assistant's way and strutted out of the store, pleased with her purchase and eager for tonight to roll around.

If Bo only saw her as an annoying, nosy, temporary employee to be tolerated in the interim, time to show him just how engaging she could be.

Six

Kathy the Koala was throwing a big party down at the water hole and everyone was invited. Fairy lights hung in the gum trees, lanterns swung from the branches, and Prue the Platypus had made fresh lemonade for everyone. There was even music blaring from the lyre bird big band. Wally was having a great time, then Kaz asked him to dance and the party got even better.

Bo Bradford's blog.

Tahnee caught sight of Bo striding across the foyer and her heart somersaulted. He looked incredible in an ivory silk shirt highlighting his tan, a black pinstripe suit, and a ruby tie setting off the combination to perfection. However, she'd seen fancy suits before, had dated guys who wore them before, but no guy had ever looked this good, this delicious...Saliva pooled in her mouth and she quickly swallowed. She'd gone to far too much trouble to drool all over her dress now.

Stepping out of the shadows, she fixed a smile on her face,

hoping it hid her nerves. She wanted his approval; heck, she craved it with every cell in her moisturised body.

Though Doris and Stan had done their best to reassure her she belonged, she'd never quit seeking approval of everyone around her growing up: her adoptive parents, teachers, friends. It was a major part of why she'd stayed in Stockton all these years. Familiarity bred security and for a shy, awkward kid who'd craved it her entire life it meant everything.

She knew the exact moment Bo spotted her. His feet stopped, his jaw dropped and his eyes rounded into huge, green, depthless pools.

"Wow," he breathed, his gaze starting at her silver spangly sandals and working slowly upward, lingering on her waist cinched with a diamanté heart and quickly flicking over her breasts. "You look beautiful."

His compliment affected her more than she cared to admit. For a girl who'd craved affection her whole life, hating the uncertainty of not knowing her real family, living with the fear of losing her adopted one, she'd never felt beautiful, even though Doris and Stan had done their best to assure her she was. Funny, cheeky, bold, were all terms she'd been labelled with growing up but no one called her beautiful.

Until now.

And though she knew the words probably didn't mean much to him and were simply a polite compliment from a naturally chivalrous guy, for one tiny moment she almost believed him.

More than satisfied by his stunned reaction, she said, "Don't sound so surprised," and sashayed her way across the living room toward him. He recovered enough to close his jaw, his blatant approval setting her pulse tripping as he toyed with his undone tie.

"I didn't plan on taking sticks with me tonight."

"Pardon?"

"To beat off the guys who are going to be flocking around you," he said, his hand stilling as she stopped in front of him. "And you thought tonight would be boring."

She laughed. "It certainly won't be if you keep flattering me like that. I can't wait to see you beat off all those guys."

"Just remember who you're coming home with," he said, staring into her eyes, his expression surprisingly serious.

"I'll remember," she murmured, knowing he was merely stating a fact but hating the way her heart leapt in crazy expectation.

He broke eye contact to send a venomous glare at the bow tie in his hands. "You wouldn't by any chance know how to do one of these? It's been a long time since I've worn one and I can't seem to get the hang of it."

"Here, let me," she said, taking the scrap of black silk, hoping her hands wouldn't shake as she slipped it around his neck, wishing he didn't smell so darn good.

She didn't go in for aftershave, hating the overpowering 'tickle up the nose' thing most of them gave her, but standing this close to Bo, enveloped in a subtle blend of spice and oak, she had to refrain from leaning forward and sniffing his neck like a hound.

He stiffened when her fingers accidentally brushed the soft skin at the nape of his neck and she quickly finished the task, her fingers turning all thumbs as she tied the final knot.

"Thanks." He grimaced and stuck a finger between the collar of his ivory dress shirt and his neck. "Yet another thing I don't miss about working in finance every day."

"Ties not your thing?"

He nodded. "That, and the whole mundane routine of shower and shave every morning, getting trussed up to impress, being judged because of it."

She could empathise. One of the joys of being self-employed and working from home was the freedom to bounce around without make-up and to work in her PJs if she chose.

"So you didn't thrive on the cut-throat mentality of making money?"

"What do you think?" His wry smile didn't soften his features. Instead, shadows swooped across his eyes before he banished them in a blink. "I'll never forget the look on my dad's face the morning I walked into his office and told him I was giving up the lure of the almighty dollar for writing. It was priceless."

"He approved though, right?"

Darkness descended like a heavy cloak, his expression gloomy again, and she silently cursed for spoiling the mood.

"Yeah, he did. It was Brennan who thought I was nuts but we got through it. We're mates."

Not good ones if his sour expression was any indication.

Aiming to lighten the mood, she said, "You're lucky. You're a talented guy to make the switch from finance to author. I bet your dad and your brother buy every one of your books and pass it out to the CEOs at their corporate meetings for their kids."

"You think?"

Bo's lips curved into a smile and she sent a high-five heavenward. Her plan to get the evening back on track had worked. Now, if she could keep her big mouth shut for the rest of the night, they might actually get through it without her annoying him or interrogating him or worse, flirting with him.

"I'm sure of it," she said, tapping her watch and jerking her head toward the door. "Isn't it time we left?"

Running a hand through his artistically mussed hair, he said, "Let's go."

As Tahnee stepped through the door Bo held open for her, she couldn't help but wonder if tonight might be a good opportunity to get her boss to loosen up. They'd got past the awkward post-kiss day and for the last few minutes had actually been able to hold a civil conversation. Wouldn't it be much easier if they could be friends over the next two weeks rather than a nervous employee tip-toeing around her sombre boss?

As she tried not to fall flat on her face in previously untried three inch heels, she followed him to the car, hoping tonight would be the start of a beautiful friendship…and not the end of her dream if she rubbed him up the wrong way yet again.

"Who's the babe?"

Bo stiffened, turning in time to see a copy-editor jerking his head in Tahnee's direction as he spoke to an up and coming agent. Annoyed at the guy's sleazy tone—and at himself for caring—Bo eavesdropped.

"Tahnee Lewis. Illustrator, I think," the agent said, his gaze firmly fixed on Tahnee while the two guys grinned like adolescents.

"She's hot." The copy-editor leered and for a second Bo had visions of bustling Tahnee out of here like an overprotective jerk, before he took a calming breath.

He'd brought her here. Hell, he'd practically ordered her to accompany him, yet somehow the evening wasn't turning out as he expected. He'd hoped to make polite small talk with his publisher and their affiliates, maybe talk up his latest marketing strategy, while Tahnee did what she did best: chat, schmooze, and bounce around the room like a hyperactive kid.

He'd got the latter right. She knew how to work a room, that's for sure. He'd barely introduced her when several publishers had whisked her away, plying her with drinks and goodness-knows-what promises of lucrative deals.

He should've been concerned but strangely he wasn't. If she'd tolerated his grumpy behaviour for the last two days and hadn't fled yet, instinct told him she'd stick it out. He knew her previous publisher had gone under, maybe she needed this job more than she let on?

Whatever, it was her business and unlike his inquisitive illustrator, he had no desire to stick his nose where it didn't belong.

She glanced up at that precise moment and their gazes locked across the room; he tilted his head in her direction, acknowledging her cheeky quirked eyebrow. In response, she winked and turned back to the CEO of some publishing conglomerate, leaving him with a glorious view of her bare back.

For a guy who didn't do distractions, his lungs along with his brain had seized when he'd first seen her in that knockout dress. Correction, seen her knockout body in that striking dress and by the tight band constricting his chest now—not to mention the extreme tightness in his pants—his reaction hadn't dimmed. If anything, watching her charm her way into some old dude's graces added to her appeal and it took a lot of willpower to look rather than make a run for it and hole up in his mansion like he had for the last five years.

He didn't need this.

Apart from the mistake he'd made last night in trying to teach her a lesson, he'd been doing great, viewing her as just an employee. Until he'd seen her in that dress, with her hair piled loosely on her head and subtle make-up highlighting her exquisite features, wearing her signature sassy smile and blue eyes gleaming in permanent amusement.

He'd known in that awful moment he was attracted to her

despite every self-protest to the contrary. And the knowledge had been like an annoying bug biting his ass ever since.

He watched her as she bid a gracious farewell to the old codger, smiled and nodded to others in the group, then made her way toward him with a smile that knocked the breath out of him even more, considering he'd been stupid enough to acknowledge the spark between them.

"You're not mingling much?"

"Too busy keeping an eye on you," he said, grabbing two champagne flutes from a passing waiter and handing her one.

"Jealous?" She raised a flute in his direction before taking a sip.

"Making sure you don't get too cosy with any of the opposition."

In every sense of the word. He'd never been the jealous type, yet watching Tahnee with other men, hot on the heels of the shocking realisation he wanted her, had brought out the protective cave man in him.

"You know I'm yours until the end of next week," she said, casting him a coy glance from beneath lowered lashes, a look designed to tease, a look designed to drive a man crazy if he let it.

"Lucky me."

Surprise widened her eyes, their unique blue offset perfectly by her shimmering dress.

"Be careful, Bo. That almost sounded like flirting."

He sent her a mock frown. "Me, flirting? You must be mistaken."

"You're too complex for me."

She sipped her champagne, her gaze fixed on him over the rim of her glass as he wondered if this was a good idea. If he'd lost his head once around her already, what hope did he have for restraint now he'd admitted to an attraction between them, albeit to himself?

"Actually, I'm a pretty simple guy."

She rolled her eyes and lowered her glass. "Yeah, as simple as a cryptic crossword."

"In that case, how good are you at clues?"

"Average. Why?"

"Unravel this," he said, placing his hand in the small of her back like he'd been wanting to do all night, savouring the warm, smooth skin beneath his palm, lingering for what seemed like an eternity before he gently guided her to one side. "I see my agent. Please excuse me for a moment. Perhaps you'll be ready to leave when I've finished?"

She stared at him in shock, her pupils dilated, her mouth a delectable, tempting rosebud.

Touching her wasn't the smartest thing he'd ever done and as he strode across the crowded room, he had a sneaking suspicion he had a whole repertoire of dumb moves to come.

Tahnee made a dash for the loo, grateful for the fancy room lined with mirrors and plush sofas, separate from the toilets. With her knees wobbling, she collapsed onto a gilt-edged day-bed.

This couldn't be happening.

She'd been psyching herself up all night to play the dutiful employee, to make contacts, to schmooze, to impress Bo into offering her an extension on her two week contract. And she'd been doing great until the last few minutes when her shy boss had done the biggest about-face of all time and actually flirted with her.

Not only that, he'd touched her.

A light hand on the back to move her out of the way couldn't be construed as an overture by any stretch of the imagination but the minute his palm had touched her, she'd lost all ability to think let alone speak. Heat, swift and scorching, had branded her back, sending fire racing through her body, fanning the flames of her imagination.

Could he be as attracted to her as she was to him?

And if so, how far could this go? How far could she push him before he reverted to stuffy Bo, frowning at her whenever she so much as glanced his way?

She could try the direct approach: *are you attracted to me?* Too direct.

How about extending our deadline? Too corny.

Or the worst: *I've got a crush on you so why don't we get creative together.*

They all sucked big time. To make matters worse, she hadn't handled the shock of his flirting well. She needed time to absorb the fact the guy she'd been secretly drooling over since she'd walked into his kitchen and seen that adorable crease between his brow might share a spark of interest in return. She needed time for her stomach to settle and stop with the internal cartwheels.

She stood and crossed to the mirror, fiddled with her hair, and made sure her make-up still looked presentable, wishing she had some idea what to do. However, the longer she stared at her reflection, the more her tummy tumbled so she spun away and headed for the door.

She always faced things head-on, a trait learned as a feisty third-grader when she'd taken down the biggest bully at Stockton Primary for taking a swipe at her foster parents.

Taking down a recalcitrant boss should be easy in comparison.

———

"When the hermit finally decides to leave the house, he goes all out, huh?"

Bo paused on the Opera House steps, sending Tahnee a glimmer of a smile. "It doesn't happen very often so now I'm out, better make the most of it. Don't you want to have a coffee after all?"

"Lead the way," Tahnee said, waving her hand toward the footpath leading to a string of upmarket restaurants lining the harbour. "I might even push my luck and ask for a raise while you're in this uncharacteristic carefree mood."

"Oh yeah, having a coffee is really taking a walk on the wild side." His wry grin seemed more relaxed than anything she'd seen yet. "I might even go the whole hog and order a slice of chocolate mud cake to go with it."

"A guy who likes to live dangerously. I like that."

Their gazes locked and she blushed, cursing her loose tongue for blurting out the first thing that popped into her head. She'd virtually implied she liked him and that was more information than he needed to know.

"Bet you'll like the richest chocolate cake on the eastern seaboard of Australia more."

Doubtful, she thought, knowing a mere dessert couldn't compare with the yummy treat before her, though this time she wisely kept her mouth shut. She couldn't read him in this unpredictable mood and though she wanted to push him a tad, to flirt and see where it led, she had a feeling she was playing with fire and could get burned.

After her mad dash to the loo she'd returned in a jaunty mood and had proceeded to hassle him to leave, expecting him to head straight back to the mansion and revert to his cantankerous self. Instead, he'd invited her to take a stroll along Circular Quay, one of her favourite parts of Sydney, and she'd accepted all too readily, hoping to make the most of this new, improved Bo.

"You're awfully quiet," he said, stopping at the bottom of

the steps and holding out a hand to help her down the last few.

"I thought you'd be rapt by that," she said, hesitating a fraction of a second before placing her hand in his and letting him guide her down the last few steps, her pulse accelerating at the feel of his fingers closing over hers.

"I suppose having you quiet rather than bombarding me with personal questions is unusual, and a welcome change."

He didn't sound annoyed and she searched his face, trying to get a feel for his mood by reading his expression.

"What can I say? I love a good mystery and you're so tight-lipped I can't help myself."

To her surprise, his eyes glittered with amusement rather than the usual coldness she'd come to expect when she presented him with her blunt honesty.

"Tight-lipped, huh?"

"Very."

"Well, we'll have to remedy that, won't we?"

Before she could ask how, his mouth swooped down to capture hers, shattering her with the hunger of his kiss.

She couldn't think. She couldn't move. Every cell in her body leapt to life, craving more as he deepened the kiss, his lips teasing her to match him, to challenge him, to give as well as receive.

Her knees trembled as his mouth repeatedly grazed hers, brushing her lips with agonising control when all she craved was for him to devour her.

Her body ignited and her self-control shredded as she clung to him, helpless to fight the onslaught of sensation short-circuiting her brain and as he slowly pulled away, her lips burned in the aftermath of the most explosive kiss she'd ever experienced.

"I thought we weren't supposed to do that anymore?" She

stared up at him, the kiss leaving her weak-kneed and more confused than ever.

"We weren't," he said, his voice cold and flat, at total odds with the fire burning in his eyes.

"Are you afraid someone might see the great Bo Bradford snogging in public?"

"Do I look afraid?"

No, he looked mad, angrier than she'd ever seen him, and considering his foul mood most of the time that was saying something.

Taking a deep breath, she made an instantaneous decision to tackle him head on. If she was going to get any work done for the rest of the two weeks, she needed answers, starting now.

"Don't you dare go all stuffy and self-righteous on me now." She jabbed a finger in his direction, stopping short of touching the hard chest she'd copped an all-too-brief feel of during that scintillating kiss. "You keep trying to push me away with your crabbiness but I know you want me."

She hadn't meant to put it like that but once the words had slipped out, she was somewhat grateful. Let Mr. Reclusive get himself out of this one.

He reached for her and gripped her upper arms, his fingers clamping onto her skin and flooding her body with heat.

"What do you want me to say? That you're wrong? That you're crazy? That I don't want you? Fine, I'll say it."

"Liar," she murmured, moistening her bottom lip with the tip of her tongue, enjoying the way his eyes focussed there, glowing with suppressed desire.

Sighing, he slowly raised his gaze to hers, banked heat blazing like a roaring inferno. "This is not supposed to happen. I don't want this to happen."

"It's only a kiss."

Yeah right, and she was just sketching pictures as a hobby.

"That's bull and we both know it."

His fingers slid down her arms, creating a soft trail of tingles that wouldn't quit; when he reached her hands, he held on tight. "I don't need complications in my life. I have my career and that's all that matters."

"And?"

She had a feeling he was leading up to something. If he would only get to the point before she burst.

"I can't get you out of my mind. Ever since you walked in the door you've been a distraction and tonight in that dress..." His gaze skimmed over her, lingering in all the right places as excitement skittered through her. "I know this is crazy. I know this goes against everything I've said before, but I want you. And by the way you've responded to my kisses I'd say you want me too? We've got less than two weeks, how about we make the most of it?"

Her heart thudded as his words sunk in. Bo wanted her; she should be thrilled. Yet 'making the most' of their time together could mean a lot of things and she needed it spelled out before she jumped to conclusions, another character flaw along with her perpetual nosiness.

"What are you suggesting?"

"Perhaps we set out a few ground rules?"

"Such as?"

"We strictly adhere to keep things platonic during work hours."

"What constitutes work hours?"

"Nine to five?"

"Uh-huh. And what are the other ground rules?"

His eyes never left hers and for all his cool, calculated control he could've been presenting a well constructed synopsis to his editor rather than asking her to do what she thought he was.

"Whatever happens out of work hours doesn't mess with our working relationship."

Tugging her hands free of his, she held up two fingers. "So rule two is we keep things light? No heavy expectations on either side?"

He nodded. "Rule three, this ends in a fortnight."

Tahnee stared at Bo, as stunned by his cocky proposal as his swift turnaround from testy boss to hot-to-trot.

'Done' teetered on the edge of her tongue but she hesitated. What if this spark they shared was unique? What if once they got started up, they couldn't stop? She'd never been a believer in fate but something about the intensity of their attraction, their connection on so many levels from professional to intellectual and beyond, had her wondering 'what if'.

What if there was more than a physical attraction here?

What if they were sensational together?

What if he wanted more than two weeks?

"What if two weeks with me aren't enough?" She tried to make light of it, hoping to get a laugh out of him when she hung on his answer.

He smiled but it wasn't the sexy, carefree smile she'd hoped for. Instead, it held a hint of sadness and she wondered why—or who—had made a cynic out of a guy who had the world at his feet yet shunned it.

"Two weeks will be enough."

He didn't mince words as expected and she shook her head, knowing she had to tread carefully if she didn't want to blow her dream job right here, right now, all for the chance to knock Bo off his incredible high horse.

"Thanks but no thanks." She glanced at her watch, faked a yawn and shifted her weight from side to side. "I'd really like to head back now rather than have a coffee. It's been quite a night."

"I've offended you."

He reached for her and she edged away, not wanting to give her traitorous body an opportunity to overturn the logical decision made by her head.

"You've surprised me," she corrected, knowing it would be hypocritical of her to be totally horrified by his proposal.

Hadn't she wanted to push him? To flirt with him? To make him see her as a desirable woman rather than an employee?

She'd got her wish…and how.

He opened his mouth as if to say something and she held up a hand to stave it off.

"Let's drop it. I'm tired. I want to head back, okay?"

He stared at her, embarrassment and regret mingling in his eyes and she turned away and headed for the car.

The rest of her working tenure promised to be arduous.

Seven

Wally didn't like water. He felt big and slow and couldn't swim well. But the watering hole was the quietest spot in the morning and Kaz didn't come down there. He liked having a new friend to help him with his work but he didn't like the funny looks she gave him. As for blowing kisses like she had last night...yuck!

Bo Bradford's blog.

Tahnee bounced out of bed after a surprisingly good night's sleep. No hot dreams of Bo—despite his outlandish proposal last night—no dreams period, unusual considering she often dreamt of her foster family, the same dream where she'd be in the kitchen helping Doris make apple pie and Stan would be sitting at the table, reading his newspaper while smiling at her antics.

The childless couple who'd lived in Stockton their entire lives had been great parents: supportive yet strict, encouraging yet firm, with an abundance of love straight from their big hearts. They'd welcomed her into their home and treated her like the daughter they never had and she wasn't surprised that even now, seven years after their deaths, she still dreamt about the warmth they'd created as a family.

She missed it; missed the comfort of belonging, of sharing, of knowing there was another person in the house at night. When Doris and Stan died within six months of each other— Doris of an aneurysm, Stan of diabetic complications—she'd been devastated, though losing them had been the catalyst for her to find her sisters.

"Good things always come out of bad," Doris would say and Tahnee had clung to that motto throughout the long search for her sisters. Thankfully, Doris had been right. Being reunited with Carissa and Kristen had been amazing yet a small part of her still yearned for the cosy cottage with its picket fence, warm kitchen and loving couple to fill it.

Tahnee padded across the bedroom, pulled up the Roman blinds, and blinked several times. Not from the morning sun streaming through the wide windows but from the dazzling sight greeting her: Bo, almost naked bar a par of funky red and black board-shorts, standing on the edge of the pool twenty metres away, poised to dive into the crystal clear water.

If her mouth wasn't dry from the morning-after effects of the few glasses of champagne she'd consumed last night, it certainly would be now as she stared, her gaze riveted as he swam a lazy four laps of the Olympic size pool before hoisting himself out and reaching for a towel.

In the time it took him to reach for the towel, about thirty glorious seconds, she had an unimpeded view of a bronzed, muscular body covered in beading water droplets. Thirty fantastic, illicit seconds when she ogled his broad chest covered in a light smattering of dark hair, moving lower to his firm abs, and lower to...

"Ouch!" Her head snapped back as she bumped her forehead on the glass. That'd teach her for leaning too far forward for a better look. Unfortunately, her clumsy head-clunking blew her cover as Bo glanced up and mistook her rubbing her sore forehead for a wave and waved back.

Great, now he'd think she'd been perving on him, which she had, but he didn't have to know about it.

Ready to bolt into the shower, she took a step back and caught her little toe on the corner of an armchair.

"Crap," she yelled, collapsing onto the chair and grabbing at her toe, sore forehead momentarily forgotten.

Her pinkie throbbed, her pride smarted and then she had to go and look out the window...only to find the cause of her pain grinning.

"It's not bloody funny," she muttered, knowing her glare would be lost at this range, and muttering curses a lady shouldn't know—another Doris saying—she hobbled to the bathroom without a backward glance.

"Breakfast?"

"Just coffee, thanks." Tahnee strolled toward the espresso machine as if she didn't have a care in the world, ignoring the constant ache in her toe that had subsided slightly once she'd traded her favourite red boots for pink beaded flip-flops. Another bonus of her denim fetish; jeans looked great with any footwear.

"Sure? I whip up a mean omelette."

She hadn't risked a glance at Bo yet but something in his voice told her she wouldn't be able to avoid him for long.

"After all, you can't take painkillers on an empty stomach."

Had he actually cracked a joke? Was that something in his tone amusement? She'd expected him to revert to sulky today after their cold silence on the drive home last night and a frigidly polite goodnight. Instead, here he was, commenting on her clumsiness, alluding to her perving on him, and laughing at her to boot.

"You're a real riot," she said, pouring herself a coffee while surreptitiously lifting her foot with the offending toe, mustering the fiercest glare she could.

His lips curved into a delicious smile, the type of smile that could melt a girl's heart if she weren't in pain—or determined to ignore him for his cool, calculated way of presenting what could be the most fun she'd had in ages—but she was, so he could take his smile and shove it.

"You okay?"

"No." She glared, he smiled, and her resistance wavered.

"Want me to take a look at it? Make sure it's not broken?"

"No."

"Maybe if you let me look at it, I could rub it for you? A good massage might help." His gentle coaxing sent the last of her resistance up in smoke.

"No way." The last thing she needed was his hands anywhere near her, even an innocuous appendage like a toe.

Softening her tone, she added, "It's not my ankle or my foot, it's my toe. I stubbed it, no big deal. But thanks for the offer."

"Suit yourself," he said, sliding into a seat and piling his plate with toast. "Your loss. I give a great massage."

Tahnee gulped and turned away, concentrating on her coffee rather than the thought of Bo's hands on her...all over her...

"You could've joined me for a swim."

Blinking away her erotic thoughts, she joined him at the table. "I'm not a morning person. Swimming is the last thing I'd want to do first thing."

His gaze locked on hers and for some unfathomable reason, she blushed. She never blushed. She gave cheek, she gave smart comebacks, she never blushed, but something about the way Bo looked at her, as if he knew exactly what she'd rather do first thing in the morning—with him—had heat surging into her cheeks.

"I'm sorry, by the way." He broke the tension by slathering butter and apricot jam on a piece of toast, and peanut butter on another.

"For what?"

She took a tentative sip of her steaming coffee, not liking the teasing quirk of his lips. He'd already apologised for his outlandish proposal last night and right now, he didn't look sorry for anything. In fact, he looked like a guy about to slam her with another one-liner.

"For being such a distraction."

He took a big bite of toast, chewed, and swallowed, while she ignored what he was implying.

"I must've looked pretty impressive out there for you to risk concussion and a broken toe to sneak a peek."

She spluttered, the coffee catching in her throat as she reached for a serviette—not to dab her mess but to wad into a ball and throw at his big head.

He laughed as her throw went wide, taunting her further by offering the stack of napkins to have another shot.

"You're not worth it," she said, cradling her mug in both hands and wishing it offered more of a defence against his smug smile and tauntng eyes.

"That's not what you thought half an hour ago."

He took another annoying crunch of toast while his eyes teased and challenged and begged her to fire back.

She shouldn't do this. Last night, her mind had been made up as she mulled over how to handle their situation on the way home. Her decision had been no trading quips, no flirting, no funny stuff. But he wasn't playing fair and what was a girl to do?

"I wasn't perving on you. You happened to be in my line of vision when I opened the blinds."

"Uh-huh." His grunted response implied he didn't believe her for a second.

"Besides, you weren't that impressive. I was checking out the view of the harbour beyond the pool. It's spectacular."

Totally accurate but her gaze hadn't made it to the harbour considering it had been riveted to Bo's body.

"Hmm."

Damn him, he still didn't believe her.

"Even if I was looking at you for just a second, the sight of you in shorts wouldn't send me crazy or anything. I tripped, that's all…" she finished lamely, her mouth twitching with barely suppressed laughter as he gave his best solemn nod.

"Stop it. You're not helping," she said, draining her coffee and slamming the mug down on the table.

"Helping what?" He leaned forward, his hand bringing toast to his mouth poised mid-lift.

Her anti-Bo policy. Her new, stay-professional-at-all-costs image, the new and improved Tahnee, the girl who didn't fall for guys she'd known for less than a week, especially guys who wanted to have it all.

"Forget it," she said, pushing back from the table and heading for the door, wincing when she inadvertently put extra weight on her toe. "I'm going to work."

His chuckles followed her out the door.

———

"I brought you something."

Tahnee hadn't looked up when Bo entered the office and by the set of her jaw, she was purposely ignoring him.

No problem, considering it gave him all the time in the world to study her: blonde hair caught up in some weird clip complete with pink feather, long eyelashes shading eyes the colour of Sydney Harbour on a cloudless summer day, and sensuous lips covered in a hint of shimmery gloss. Lips he'd tasted, lips that had haunted his dreams last night, lips taunting him to come back for seconds...

Now he'd finally admitted to being attracted to her, he could stand here all day and watch her, admiring the curve of her breasts outlined clearly in another tight T-shirt, pale blue today, and her long legs encased in faded denim. She was the whole package, from the tips of her layered hair to her pinkie toe which even at this distance he could see had swelled to almost double its size.

Struck by how painful the toe looked, he stepped forward and held out the icepack he'd brought when hit by a pang of conscience after she hobbled from the kitchen.

"Put this on your toe. It'll help with the swelling."

She glanced up and rather than glimpsing annoyance as he'd expected, she surprised him yet again with a genuine teasing sparkle in her eyes.

"Is this your idea of a peace offering? A lousy pack of frozen peas wrapped in a dish cloth?"

He shrugged and made to turn away. "Fine, if you don't want it—"

"Thanks, I'll take it." She made a frantic grab at the ice pack, which told him exactly how much pain she must be in.

"You should've told me it was this bad." He sat next to her, picked up her foot, and placed it on a cushion with the ice pack on it.

"You would've laughed at me anyway."

She winced as he readjusted the pack, biting down on her bottom lip, and he felt like a jerk for laughing off her pain earlier.

"You sure it's not broken?"

She shook her head, setting aside her sketchpad and charcoals and regarding him with an intensity that had him squirming. "No, because I've broken it before. This is just a bad stub. I'll live, which is more than I can say for you."

"What did I do?"

Her stare wavered and for a second he glimpsed vulnerability in her eyes. "Last night. That kiss and your stupid ground rules."

He aimed for levity, not knowing where this was going and hoping he wouldn't find out. "You're going to kill me over one kiss? I'd hate to see what would happen if we went the whole way."

To his amazement, she blushed. Super-confident women with smart mouths didn't blush. Then again, he'd been out of circulation for a while, what did he know?

Her drawn-out exasperated sigh indicated she didn't appreciate his humour. "I've been thinking about what you said last night. I've been teasing you a fair bit, trying to get you to loosen up so I don't blame you entirely for wanting the fling thing."

"The fling thing?" He tried to keep a straight face but his lips twitched the harder he tried to fight it.

"See? That's exactly what I mean." She pointed at his mouth. "You didn't do that when I first arrived. In fact, you're the stuffiest, uptight guy I've ever met. But since last night you've been smiling and teasing and laughing and it's too hard."

"Too hard?"

"Keeping things platonic. Not flirting, not kissing, and the rest." She paused, her mouth softening, and it took all his willpower not to lean across the couch, haul her into his arms and do exactly what she didn't want him to do. "What made you do an about-face anyway?"

He'd been contemplating the same question all night considering sleep had eluded him. Several reasons had sprung to mind, most of them involving his reclusive lifestyle but he'd known they were a crock.

Simply, Tahnee had wrought a change without him realising and it felt good. It felt downright fantastic. Why shouldn't he have a little fun with a beautiful woman for the first time in ages? He worked hard enough. He deserved it.

And it wasn't like anyone would discover his secret because of it.

"Honestly?"

She pinned him with an astute stare. "It's the only way to be."

Maybe he was making a huge mistake in opening up to her? Maybe it would be inviting trouble when his world had finally righted itself?

At that moment, he didn't care. He and his pal Wally had been holed up by themselves for far too long. If Wally could let Kaz into his life, he could take a chance on Tahnee.

"I've been living like a hermit for years. My work is my focus. I've dated occasionally, done the obligatory socialising with work colleagues at publishing functions, but other than that I've deliberately kept to myself. Moira was unobtrusive and work focussed. Then you came along and in less than a few days, I'm thinking along very unprofessional lines."

"Oh." One, short syllable uttered on a soft breath as she sank back against the cushions, looking decidedly sheepish.

"That honest enough for you?"

Saying out loud what he'd been thinking all night felt like a weight rolled off his shoulders. Work had always been enough for him, the imaginary world of his characters so much more appealing than the crazy world he lived in. Yet something had changed last night the minute he'd seen Tahnee in that dress and he knew he couldn't go back to hiding behind his work no matter how much he wanted to.

"Aren't you going to say anything? Guys aren't used to

opening up like that and you're leaving me flapping in the breeze. The least you can do is reassure me."

Her cheeky smile kicked in. "You don't need reassurance. I think you got all the reassurance you need when I responded to your kiss last night."

"It was pretty spectacular, wasn't it?"

"Too right."

They stared at each other, the same sexual tension from yesterday stretching taut between them, and as her lips parted in a tiny O, the blood from his brain rushed south.

"You know those unprofessional thoughts I mentioned a second ago?"

"Yeah?" She leaned forward a fraction and he wondered if she knew what an appealing picture she presented: beautiful, eager, wanting.

"I'm having some of them right now."

She smiled, a coy curving of her lips designed to tease, to tantalise. "Maybe I was being a bit harsh in wanting to tell you to shove your offer?"

"Maybe," he said, unable to keep his hands off her a minute longer, resting his hand on her ankle and tracing slow circles around her jutting bones with his thumb.

She shivered, a blissful expression illuminating her face as she stared at his hand, mesmerised. "Perhaps I should amend it?"

"Perhaps." He increased the pressure, sliding his hand downward to cup her foot, his thumb pressing into her instep.

Her eyelids fluttered shut for a brief moment and he smiled, enjoying her obvious pleasure at his touch. If she liked his foot massages, wait until he started on the rest of her. Not that he was cocky but something had shifted between them in the last few minutes and he hoped she felt half as good as he did after their honest chat.

Her eyes flew open and she fixed him with that guileless

stare only she did so well. "I need to finish drawing this scene otherwise we'll never make deadline. Thanks for the massage."

She all but jerked her foot out of his hand, leaving him no option but to replace it gently on the cushion, refasten the ice pack, and head for his desk.

"I guess I should be applauding your work ethic," he said, sitting and glancing at his inbox with little interest, wishing he still held her delicate foot in his hand. Pathetic, considering he'd take whatever physical contact he could get at this point.

"Don't applaud me yet. You haven't seen the finished result of the second last chapter."

As if to prove a point she propped her sketchpad vertically on her lap, effectively screening him out.

"I trust you," he said, opening the current chapter he'd been working on, wondering if he'd be able to get anything done now his libido had been hot-wired into action and all he could focus on was the luscious woman sitting on the couch opposite.

He trusted her.

Himself, not so much.

———

Tahnee didn't know whether to be insulted or flattered by Bo's attention. Now he'd turned nice and normal on her, she almost wished he'd revert to cold and stuffy. That guy she could handle. This new, improved version of Bo was driving her insane.

She shouldn't even contemplate what he'd suggested last night but the longer she sat here and the tension between them stretched to breaking point, she knew her holier-than-thou intentions might not be the best action to take.

So what if she had a wild, passionate fling with Bo and it ended in two weeks? She'd be bored, let-down, alone, three things she was right now without the promise of sizzling sex thrown in.

For she had no doubt the sex would be amazing. If he kissed like a dream, he'd have all the moves downpat. Not to mention he didn't get out much and if he hadn't had sex in a while...her cheeks heated at the thought, not to mention the throb of her regions that hadn't seen much action in a long time.

Nibbling her bottom lip, she drew a pouch on Wally rather than Kaz, scrubbing furiously when she realised her concentration was shot. How could she focus on sketching cute animals when Bo sat behind his desk, looking like a sexy, ruffled, eccentric guy and she couldn't keep her eyes off him?

Ironic, she'd wanted to draw him out of his shell, tease him a little, get him to notice her. Last night he'd come out of his shell well and truly, smashing it to smithereens along the way.

"What's up?" He looked up from his PC screen and she dropped her gaze but not quickly enough by his smug grin.

"Nothing, just trying to get a grumpy expression for Wally and thought you'd be good inspiration for that."

He sat back, folded his hands and placed them behind his head, his cocky posture serving to accentuate his broad chest, the soft cotton of his black T-shirt pulled taut across it.

"But I'm not grumpy any more, remember? You've seen to that."

She huffed, determinedly staring at her sketchpad rather than his smirk. She'd always used a smart mouth and quick wit to get the upper hand in any situation. It had served her well, the perfect self-protective mechanism to hide her vulnerability at not fitting in or not belonging. After the early years when she'd done anything and everything to please Doris and Stan, taking a long time to learn she didn't have to as they loved her unconditionally anyway, she'd never been able to shake the habit.

It explained why she hadn't shut up since she'd walked through Bo's door. For a guy who had it all—the perfect house, the dream job, the charmed life—he wouldn't have the foggiest idea how a defenceless orphan scared of her own shadow felt or what that girl needed to do to cope with the uncertainty of having her world upended by circumstances beyond her control.

Yet now, her quick wit had deserted her along with every ounce of common sense she'd ever possessed if the persistent throbbing in her body the moment he glanced her way was any indication.

"No comeback?"

She ignored his taunt. "No time. Must work."

"Okay," he said, his low chuckles washing over her, teasing her to join in whatever game he was playing.

Ignoring the urge to glance up, she focussed on her sketches until her eyes blurred. She could switch off her mind, ignore her instincts and try to concentrate on work. Or she could get real and face facts. She was attracted to Bo. More attracted than she'd ever been to any other guy before. She could feign indifference for the remainder of her time here.

Or she could have the wildest fling of her life.

The choice was hers and her gut churned with a potent mixture of anticipation and dread: anticipation of what having a fling with a spectacular guy like Bo would be like, dread for the consequences.

For as much as she'd like to pretend she could handle a fling, it wasn't her style. Never had been, never would be. Every guy she'd been out with had been sized up for F potential: future, father, fun, and forever. Not that she expected Bo to live up to anything but the fun part of her F equation but what if she added another F to the list in the form of a fool?

Forever type of girls always ended up feeling like fools when they hoped for futures that weren't there or never could be. Hopefully, she'd be too busy concentrating on the fun part to worry about the rest.

She laid down her charcoal and flexed her toes gingerly, pleased when pain didn't shoot up her foot. She had to get out of here now, before she let her gut rule her head, threw caution to the wind and accepted Bo's crazy offer.

"I'll see you later," she said, not looking in his direction as she hobbled for the door.

"What happened to work?"

"Screw it."

"Let me know if you need anything," he said, his tone low and cajoling, and she wished his soft chuckles didn't have the same effect on her as his sensuous touch.

Eight

Wally had never felt so out of sorts. He usually spent most of his day digging in the dirt but not today. Kaz had chatted a lot and to Wally's surprise he liked it. In fact, he liked Kaz. His tummy didn't feel so funny when she stared at him now and he even looked forward to later when she might blow him another goodnight kiss.

Bo Bradford's blog.

Tahnee had never been a clock-watcher. She worked her own hours, eating when she felt hungry, taking a break when she needed. Never in all her working years had she experienced anything like this intense compulsion to check her watch every five minutes, silently cursing when the hands didn't move fast enough for her liking.

It was all *his* fault.

She propped up her sketchbook, using it as an effective screen to surreptitiously check out the object of her discontent. For a savvy career woman, she'd let her brains turn to mush courtesy of her stupid hormones.

Was she actually considering accepting his crazy ground rules for a fling? She must be nuts. Maybe all the years sketching fictional characters had sucked her into believing she could be a naughty princess for a week or two and have some fun?

"Is something wrong?"

She jumped. Great, he'd sensed her stare without looking up from his computer screen. So much for subtlety.

"No, just thinking."

His fingers stopped clattering and he glanced at her, a knowing gleam in his eyes. "Thought I could hear the wheels turning from here. Thinking about anything in particular?"

She wracked her brain for a quick excuse and made a mental grab for the first thought that popped into her head. "Fairytales."

He pushed back from the desk, folded his arms and fixed her with an amused 'this is going to be good' stare.

"You're thinking about fairytales?"

"Uh-huh, just likening what you write to fairytales, that sort of thing," she said, inordinately pleased with her quick save.

"Wally's more of a realist. He doesn't always get a happy ending."

"Yeah, but the concept is basically the same. You bring joy to kids by inventing happy stories. Fairytales do that too."

She sounded so convincing he'd never know she'd been casting him in the role of a bad prince about to rip off her cape and make all her dreams come true.

"I'm looking forward to knock-off time too," he said, grinning at her like someone who had his cake and was about to eat it too—in one huge gorging feast.

"What?"

"You tug at your right ear when you're fibbing so I guess your mind isn't on my stories and more along the lines of what we discussed over lunch? About you taking me to your favourite spot in Sydney for dinner?"

Tahnee dropped her right arm in record time, unaware she'd been fiddling with her earring and sent him her best haughty glare.

"Perhaps you'd like me to add mind-reader to the list of your attributes, alongside massive ego?"

His grin widened. "You've made a list?"

Making an unladylike sound somewhere between a snort and a curse, she rattled the pages of her sketchbook in his general direction. "I'm getting back to work. I suggest you do the same."

Silence greeted her snooty proclamation. Surprising, considering he always had to have the last word.

"You're right. Concentrating will make time fly and we both know how much we want six o'clock to roll around."

Tahnee kept her eyes trained on a cute pic of Kaz and Wally sparring, knowing she should ignore him but unable to do so. "Dream on."

"I've been doing plenty of that and now I'm looking forward to the real thing."

His silky tone taunted her, begging her to respond, to match wits with him, and a small part of her loved it. She admired a guy's body like the next woman but give her a glimpse of well-rounded intellect combined with a killer sense of humour and she was a goner.

She finally looked up, aware that looking at him was infinitely more interesting than her drawings. The same drawings she'd been staring at for the last fifteen minutes in an effort not to look at him.

"For a grumpy recluse, you've turned into a charmer pretty darn quick."

His slow, sexy smile kicked her pulse into double time and

she forced herself to stay seated rather than drape herself over his desk like she wanted to.

"Charmer, huh? You must have a lot of faith in my flirting abilities."

"Faith, stupidity, they're close relations."

Any other guy would've wilted under her 'I don't give a damn' tone and stare. But Bo wasn't any other guy, which is why she needed a cold shower, a lobotomy, or a combination of both.

"You know I'm teasing, right? I like to get a rise out of you." The glimmer of amusement in his eyes faded. "And you know I have no expectations, right?"

As if. Guys always expected more than she was willing to give.

"So you're telling me you don't want more than that kiss at the Opera House?"

He held out his hands as if showing her he had no tricks up his sleeves. "No expectations, see? No preconceptions, no assumptions, just a vain hope you'll take pity on a guy who doesn't get out much and maybe ravish me one night in my sleep?"

Laughter bubbled out and she shook her head. She didn't stand a chance against this guy. He'd crumbled her defences quicker than she could erect them.

"You never know your luck," she said, wondering if he felt the same sense of impending inevitability hanging over them, the sense that no matter what they said or how much they danced around each other, they'd end up having sex anyway.

"On that note, I'm going for a run." He stood, giving her a perfect view of the body she'd been ogling every second she could. She hated exercise but if swimming and jogging could produce those sorts of results, he'd be a great advertisement to get off the couch. "To burn off all the excess energy I've got."

She registered his meaning but didn't acknowledge it. Her

head ached from all the witty repartee and the sooner he removed his hot bod and sharp mind, the better.

"Have fun." She waved and pretended to add a few flourishes to her sketch, knowing she wouldn't do another stroke of work once he left. Instead, she had a date with a razor, exfoliator and moisturiser, just in case.

"We will."

She thought she'd imagined his murmured response laden with promise until she glanced up and caught his meaningful glance before he strolled out the door.

"Not tonight dear, I have a headache," Tahnee muttered at her reflection, smirking at the hypocrisy of her statement.

She had a headache because she'd spent too long dithering over her wardrobe, followed by an inordinately long time in front of the mirror trying to achieve a no make-up look with make-up. She rarely bothered with the stuff back home, hence her extended stay at the mirror trying to curl lashes, prime for foundation, and contour cheekbones.

As for 'not tonight', she'd already made up her mind on that score. She was sticking to the fun part of her F motto whatever that may entail.

Smacking her lips together after applying a sheer layer of gloss, she reached for the hairdryer in another first. She never, ever, blow-dried her hair, preferring to let it dry naturally. The only time she had silky smooth hair was after a visit to the hairdresser where they did the job for her. She was a low maintenance kind of gal and preferred it that way, which explained her clueless state now as she tussled with hot, blasting air and a round spiked hairbrush.

After five angst-filled minutes and several close calls with burnt strands and frizz-control-serum that obviously didn't deliver what it promised, she laid the hairdryer down in defeat and gathered her hair up in a high ponytail. Not the most seductive of looks but hey, she'd gone way past her tolerance limit with the eyelash curler anyway.

Her cell rang and she knew Carissa must've used every ounce of her limited willpower to wait this long to call for an update following their texting session last night.

Tahnee hit the answer button. "Hey, Sis. What, no snazzy text tonight?"

"Tell me everything."

Tahnee plopped onto the bed and propped her feet up, grinning as she caught sight of her pinkie toe that had finally returned to normal proportions and remembering how she'd injured it in the first place.

"Firstly, how are the kids? I miss the munchkins."

Carissa sighed and Tahnee knew she'd be torn. Her sister loved Molly and Jack more than life itself and could spend hours talking about their latest achievements from mastering maths to starting on solids. But she loved a good gossip session too and right now she'd want to get down to the good stuff.

"Molly's fine. She's spelling champion of second grade as of today and Jack managed to ingest more mashed pumpkin today than wear it. And before you ask, Brody's fine too. Now, spill it. I want to hear everything."

Smoothing an imaginary crease from her denim skirt—another attempt to dress things up tonight considering she never wore skirts and had only brought this one after incessant nagging from Carissa—she answered in her best naïve voice.

"The job's great. I'm illustrating two new characters for the latest book, which is due real soon and—"

"Don't make me drive down there."

Tahnee laughed. She wouldn't put anything past Carissa and her quest for gossip.

"Okay, okay. I was going to call you earlier anyway but got tied up getting ready for dinner."

"Dinner? With anyone special?" Carissa's tone lowered an octave, the same tone she used on Brody to coerce him into doing something he didn't want to do.

"If you call my boss special," Tahnee said, her voice deliberately bland. "Personally, I'd call him a big pain in the butt but hey, that's just me."

Tahnee knew she'd pushed Carissa to the limit and waited for the fallout. It was such a blast winding her up.

"Tahnee Lewis, if you don't tell me what's going on right this instant I'll set Daisy on you."

Tahnee chuckled, knowing Daisy, Stockton's octogenarian and resident matchmaker, would have a field day with her and Bo. After all, look at the interference she'd run on Carissa and Brody, all but pushing the two of them together.

"Okay, you got me. You want the goss? Here it is. Bo is drop dead gorgeous with a hot bod and fabulous smile. He has a great sense of humour and can match my comebacks, but the best bit? He gives great foot massages."

Silence greeted her for all of two seconds before Carissa squealed. "You've known the guy less than a week and he's already touched your feet? Wow, T. You're a fast mover."

"Don't worry, that's all he's touched."

Though not for much longer if she had any say in it. "He's a decent guy and I'm enjoying working with him. He was super shy and grumpy to begin with but has loosened up a lot." Understatement of the year. "It's a bonus that he's easy on the eye and can lighten up when needed."

"Uh-oh."

"What?"

"You never sing a guy's praises. You always talk down your dates."

"And your point?"

Carissa paused, obviously choosing her words very carefully. "You must think this guy is pretty special to talk him up, especially to me."

"Maybe he is."

Tahnee opted for the truth as always. She may be many things—flighty, vivacious, with a hankering for gossip—but she knew she wouldn't be contemplating having a fling with Bo unless she liked him. A lot. Besides, if she couldn't confide in her sister, she'd go nuts.

"Wow." Another pause, before Nina rushed on. "I'm happy for you. Enjoy yourself, have fun with this guy, but be careful, okay?"

"Careful's my middle name," Tahnee said, and they both guffawed.

A knock sounded on her bedroom door and she bolted upright, almost knocking her head on the lamp. Jeez, she'd end up with a serious injury by the end of the fortnight at this rate.

"Is that him?"

Tahnee smoothed down her skirt and slipped into flat sandals, her favourite black ones with the gold, turquoise and emerald embroidery. "Uh-huh."

"At the risk of sounding like a prudish overprotective sister, why is he knocking on your bedroom door?"

Tahnee smiled, opened the door and held up a finger to Bo, asking for a minute. "How do you know I'm in my bedroom?"

Carissa blew a raspberry. "As a mother, I have eyes in the back of my head, remember? And radar that extends all the way to Sydney."

Tahnee snickered. "Bye, Carissa."

"Bye, Sis. Love you. And be careful."

Tahnee disconnected, to find the incredible green eyes of the guy she hoped would rock her world tonight staring at her with blatant interest.

"Sorry about that. My sister Carissa checking up on me. You're right on time," she said, thrusting out her hip and smoothing a hand over her shimmering green top and tight denim skirt, a teasing move designed to entice, enjoying the appreciative once-over he gave her.

"You look great," he said, his sexy smile setting her pulse racing.

"Glad you noticed, considering I've gone to way too much trouble with my make-up, though I guess the teeny-bopper ponytail sort of spoils the whole look, huh?"

She was babbling, her mouth running at a million miles an hour, anything to cover her nerves and the fact a whole farm of butterflies flapped madly in her belly.

"I like the ponytail. It's cute." He reached out and tugged it, a gentle, barely-there pull that set her scalp tingling along with the rest of her. "As for the make-up, I appreciate the effort you went to but you don't need it. You're gorgeous without it."

"Sweet-talker," she said, his gallant words more than making up for his grouchy behaviour in the first few days.

"So where are we going?" His smile slipped and his shoulders stiffened imperceptibly, and she wondered if he'd always been this anti-social or it was an after-effect of too much schmoozing in his finance days.

"Don't sound so enthusiastic," she said, hoping he'd go for her idea and actually loosen up enough to enjoy it.

"You know I don't get out much. Guess I'm concerned what your version of a casual dinner is?"

"Don't worry, my anti-social friend. We're going somewhere quiet so it shouldn't offend your sensibilities," she said in a fake posh voice and tilted her nose in the air, peeking at him from beneath her lashes.

He chuckled. "In that case, how can I refuse?"

"I knew you couldn't," she said, her expression smug as

she grabbed her purse and hustled him out the door. "It's part of my charm."

"What? Guys not saying no to you?"

"There are no guys. Hasn't been for a while, actually."

"Same here."

For one, long moment, they connected. Here was a guy who knew about loneliness, self-inflicted by the sounds of it, and as much as he touted the whole 'a creative genius needs his privacy' spiel, she still didn't understand why a gorgeous, intelligent guy wouldn't have a string of drooling women at his feet.

"Well, I guess this get-up is wasted then." She waved a hand at her outfit and this time, his stare lingered in all the right places, particularly her legs slathered in moisturiser. "You not dating guys for a while and all."

"Are you always this smart-mouthed?"

"You like my mouth?"

She puckered up and for a moment she could see the gleam in his eyes as if he was tempted to teach her a lesson, a very sexy lesson she hoped.

"A lady never fishes for compliments."

"And a gentleman wouldn't need prompting to pay them."

She shut the door and flounced ahead of him, their banter buoying her mood. With a little luck, tonight would be fun with a capital F.

Nine

Wally hadn't eaten under the stars for ages. By this time of night he'd usually burrowed in, having a nice hot cup of cocoa and reading his favourite book. Not tonight. Wally felt confused. He liked having Kaz around. He liked having a new friend. But she kept surprising him. Kaz had taken him on a picnic to his favourite watering hole and she'd been extra nice to him but all he could think about was going home to bed. And he wasn't even tired!

Bo Bradford's blog.

"Hope you like anchovies." Tahnee rummaged through the picnic basket, searching for the little glass jar housing one of her favourite acquired tastes.

Though her question sounded innocuous enough, she waited with bated breath for Bo's answer. She'd asked a few guys the same question and it had become a screening tool used to weed out the good from the bad. The good guys always responded in the affirmative or were open to trying them and they had more than a few dates. The duds hated anchovies and proceeded to tell her why or treat her like a weirdo for liking them.

"Are you kidding? I love them."

Relieved, she found the jar and held it aloft like a gold medal winner. "Good. I didn't know if you would or not so I brought a jar rather than slathering them on the pizza rolls."

"Smart girl," he said, his simple praise making her glow.

"So you don't mind the picnic?"

He smiled and his approval lit her from within. "Mind? This is great. I can't remember the last time I've been here let alone had a picnic."

"This is one of my favourite spots when I visit Sydney."

She stared at the lights twinkling on Sydney Harbour, enjoying the hustle and bustle of a warm summer evening. The Manly ferries jostled for space alongside pleasure-cruisers, water taxis transported passengers, and the dinner cruises were packed with happy people toasting each other on deck. Though she loved Stockton, Sydney had a vibe she adored and for her it centred on the water.

"I thought you were a born and bred country girl?"

"Stockton's not country. Though I guess a city slicker like you would think that."

As for the born and bred part, he had no idea. Determined not to go down the miserable road of her early childhood, she said, "You've always been a Sydney boy?"

"Yes."

No elaboration, no explanation. Guess she wasn't the only one who didn't want to talk about the past.

"Here, have another mini quiche." She thrust the container holding the most exquisite sun-dried tomato and feta quiches she'd ever tasted under his nose, hoping the food would distract him from the awkward silence.

"Real men don't eat quiche," he said, taking two anyway.

"Trust me, you're real enough."

Tahnee paused, hand midway between mouth and container. Had she just verbalised her thought?

"I'll take that as a compliment," he said, raising his mini-quiche in a toast and she blushed, thankful for the descending dusk and quickly stuffing a quiche into her mouth before she said anything else incriminating.

They ate in companionable silence and she wondered when she'd last felt this relaxed in a guy's company. Usually, first dates entailed sitting at a restaurant across the table from some over-confident jerk with a high opinion of himself, being bored senseless by stories of his football prowess or the size of his portfolio.

Though technically, this wasn't a first date. They hadn't spelled it out as such but the way they'd been flirting earlier today and hot on the heels of his proposal, he'd have to be thick as a brick wall not to realise she was coming around to his way of thinking. She wouldn't fall into his arms without a prelude though.

"You didn't have to go to all this trouble," he said and she startled, wondering if he'd read her mind.

"No trouble. Picking up the phone and ordering a gourmet picnic isn't exactly rocket science." Figuring out what to wear had been the hard part requiring a degree.

"What I meant to say was I know we had that strange conversation this morning about rules and flings and stuff but don't feel like I expect anything from you."

He folded his forearms and rested them on his knees, leaning forward to pin her with a steady stare. "I put you in an awkward position by kissing you and then following up with that not-so-classy proposition, and I'm sorry."

"Don't be," she said, her heart sinking.

Once she'd got over her initial reticence—and finally admitted she liked him enough to ignore her previous reservations and take what she could for the short time they had together—she wasn't sorry, but it was pretty obvious he was and was trying to back-pedal faster than a runaway bride.

"You know I'm attracted to you because that's a given considering what's happened so far, but I don't want to jeopardise our working relationship."

His level-headed rationale made perfect sense and she'd considered the same drawbacks of getting involved with her boss. But she couldn't help it. She'd never been this drawn to a guy before and a huge part of her wanted to throw caution to the wind and jump him, right here, right now.

"I've only just found you," he added, softening the blow with another sexy smile. "And I don't want to lose such a talented illustrator."

He wasn't making this easy on her. When in doubt, she opted for bluntness. "So you are attracted to me, right?"

"I've just said so, haven't I?"

"Don't answer my question with a question." She sounded exceedingly snippy and lightened up with a tremulous smile. "You enjoyed the kiss at the Opera House?"

"It was amazing."

His reluctant admission came out a half-hearted mutter but she couldn't blame him. He was trying to defuse their situation, she was trying to inflame it.

"And correct me if I'm wrong, but didn't you propose some clear ground rules if we were to get involved, one of which was to not let anything interfere with our work?"

"I did." His eyes glowed emerald in the dusk and in that moment, she knew she had him. Figuratively at least; she was working hard on the literally part.

"Okay then. Stop back-pedalling." She leaned back on her elbows, going for the knock-out move—chest out, hair toss, seductive smile—the basic equivalent of 'take me'. "What's the problem? From where I'm sitting, things are looking pretty good."

His gaze raked over her, lingering on her breasts, skimming her legs, focussing on her mouth. "They look sensational from where I'm sitting."

"In that case, what are we waiting for?"

She sat up and began packing up the remnants of their picnic, eager to get back to the mansion before he changed his mind.

Bo laughed and helped her stack the plates and containers. "What about dessert?"

"You're looking at it," she murmured, caressing his cheek with the briefest of touches designed to entice.

"Good, because I'm still starving," he said, capturing her hand, raising it to his lips and planting a scorching kiss on her palm, sending the last of their doubts and second-guessing up in smoke.

Bo flicked on the light switch, dumped the picnic basket on the kitchen table, and cast a desperate glance around the room in search of more camouflage.

The picnic basket had been good while it lasted but now he couldn't hold it in front of him anymore, he was exposed. Having the hard-on to end all hard-ons made him feel like a randy teenager about to lose his virginity when Tahnee strolled into the kitchen, all five foot seven of perfection.

"So...here we are again."

She propped against the table in a deliberate provocative pose, similar to how she'd conquered his lingering resistance at the Point. Her round breasts thrust forward, the hard nubs of her nipples prominent through the silky top that shimmered from basic green to cerulean when she moved, her lips pouted, and her shaded eyes glittered with seductive promise.

He was a goner.

"Would you like something to drink?"

She shook her head and tugged on the band holding her ponytail up, freeing her hair to fall in a glossy golden curtain. He made a sound, a gasp or a groan he wasn't sure, and her lips curved in a sexy smirk.

"I thought you wanted dessert?"

She took a step forward and his gaze riveted to her leg, the way her hip and knee flexed in perfect synchronicity, how her thigh muscle tightened against the denim and how smooth the skin extending from her knee to ankle looked. He'd always been a leg man and Tahnee's didn't disappoint.

"I do," he said, shifting behind a chair before she spotted exactly how much.

"Good. I'm partial to chocolate myself."

He watched her stroll across the kitchen, flick on the kettle, fill a bowl with par-boiled water and place a chocolate topping bottle in it.

"I didn't think I owned any chocolate topping?"

"You don't. I asked the gourmet place to drop it around specifically when they brought the picnic."

So she'd actually meant dessert rather than...*dessert*. Maybe it had been too long since he'd done this because he had no idea what was going on and he was tying himself up in knots trying to figure it out.

"Slight problem. I don't have any ice cream."

She eyeballed him, her gaze hotter than molten lava, her smile slow and sexy. "Who said anything about needing ice cream?"

Bo stared at her, blood pounding through his body as he wavered between shock and anticipation. Call him boring but he'd always been a straight-up kind of guy when it came to sex. Sure, he liked mixing up positions and he loved oral but he'd never tried eating food off each other.

Looked like he was about to expand his education.

She laughed at his expression, which he tried to school into cool but probably looked as dumbfounded as he felt. "Don't worry. The chocolate is about as kinky as it gets."

He didn't want to know about her past. The thought of her with other guys made him oddly jealous when he had no right to be. But the minute she pulled out the topping bottle and said it wasn't for ice cream, a sense of inadequacy crept over him.

He'd kick himself in the morning if he screwed this up but he had to know what she expected from him. The topping might be fun to try but he'd draw the line at swinging from the chandeliers.

"At the risk of sounding like a jerk, I'm not sure what you expect apart from the chocolate thing," he said, hating the amusement in her eyes and feeling like a fool.

"Relax," she said, picking up the bottle, testing it for temperature and apparently unsatisfied—what he would be if he mucked this up—submerged it again. "Want to know a secret?"

"Uh...sure."

Schmuck. Now she'd be telling him goodness knows what about her sexual past and he'd know he couldn't match up. Hell, his hard-on wilted just thinking about it.

"I've never done this before."

"What?"

For a startling second he thought she meant she was a virgin and there was no way he'd be responsible for possibly ruining the best working relationship he'd ever had.

She nibbled on her bottom lip, a nervous habit he'd noticed, and a small part of him was glad her uncertainty matched his.

"I've never done the chocolate topping thing before. I read about it in this really hot romance novel and it's been something I wanted to try ever since."

"Oh."

Why would she trust him, a guy she barely knew, to indulge in this particular fantasy with? Was it because of the ground rules they'd set, about the non-permanence of their arrangement? Even so, they hadn't even had sex yet and she was getting into some pretty personal stuff. He should be flattered by her trust but it left him more confused than ever.

"You're wondering why I'm doing this when we haven't... done it yet?"

"Yeah," he said, grateful for her honesty.

He'd never met a woman so blunt before and it was a refreshing change.

She looked him straight in the eye. "Because I think we have a connection. Because I wouldn't even consider sleeping with you unless we didn't. Because I trust you. And best of all, you have the perfect criteria for using chocolate topping and I saw most of it this morning when you got out of the pool."

Her simple honesty made him feel ten feet tall and he crossed the space separating them, held out his arms and stifled a sigh when she slid into them.

She'd be gone in less than two weeks, he had to remember that. He didn't do connections, he didn't want the emotional links that bound two people together. When she'd mentioned a connection, he knew she was talking about the physical attraction they'd already discussed. That, he could do. As for anything else, he'd make sure he retreated behind his well-maintained privacy once this was over.

If their working relationship worked out—and he had a strong feeling it would—Tahnee would head back to her home town and they'd work remotely. His agent had already mentioned she usually worked that way and now he could see it as the perfect solution for both of them. Have a short time to connect on a physical and professional level, and maintaining a work relationship from afar after it.

Yeah, it could work, and thankfully she'd gone for his rule about nothing beyond the two weeks. He had it made. Then why the niggle of doubt he was in over his head?

"You think I'm a freak, don't you?" She murmured against his chest and he pulled back, placing a finger under her chin and tilting her face up.

"I think you're incredible." He feathered his thumb along her bottom lip, loving the way her pupils dilated and her lips parted on a soft sigh. "I've never met anyone like you before."

Her lips curved upward, slowly, tentatively. "That's a good thing?"

"You bet," he said, using every ounce of self control to lower his head slowly and graze her lips with his when he wanted to devour her.

"You kiss real good for a hermit," she murmured, trailing her lips along his jaw before returning to his mouth.

"You'd be surprised what other stuff us hermits are good at." He backed her up against the bench, sliding his hands into her hair, savouring the silky texture while pressing into her, his hard erection against her soft pelvis.

"This is it. Last chance to back out, change ground rules, come to your senses, whatever," he said, lifting her hair off the nape of her neck and nibbling his way downward towards her collarbone.

"I'll take the whatever."

His head lifted, their gazes locked, and time stood still with the heady anticipation of what they were about to do.

"Come with me." He grabbed her hand and headed for the door, unable to stand one more minute of this torture, standing here deliberating with clothes on when he wanted her naked and moaning in his arms, and to be buried deep within her.

"We forgot the chocolate," she said, keeping in perfect step with him and not stopping for a second.

"Later."

They had all night. They had the rest of the week and the next and he intended to make every minute count with the woman who'd made him lose his mind.

She laughed in wild abandon as they made a run for his room, their feet barely touching the polished floor boards.

"Lucky that toe's all better," he said, fumbling with the door knob for a second before flinging open his bedroom door and they tumbled into the room together.

"Yeah, must've been your magic touch." She tugged him to her for a swift, passionate kiss, igniting the raging inferno of need simmering between them in a second.

"You ain't seen nothing yet," he murmured, working his way down the elegant column of her neck to her tantalising cleavage that had teased him all night.

She arched into him, offering her breasts and her body, and he wondered how on earth he'd got so lucky.

"I could do this all night long." He licked his way across the swell of her breasts spilling out of her bra, unzipping the silky top with fingers turned into thumbs, wanting to prolong the unveiling of her beauty like a master with an exquisite painting but knowing he didn't have that much patience. He wanted to see her, all of her; to feast his eyes, to slake his thirst for her.

The scrap of top pooled at her feet and his lips slowed momentarily as he traced the outline of her nipples through the sheer black lace bra with his fingertip.

"You are so sexy," he said, replacing his fingertip with his mouth, suckling her, fired by her moans and his need.

"More." She gasped as he lifted his head and blew on her dampened skin, watching her nipples pebble into tighter, firmer buds.

He smiled, knowing he'd never seen anything so tempting as the blonde goddess before him, her hair tumbling in disarray around her shoulders, her breasts clearly visible through the bra, and her swollen lips parted and asking for more.

"Stop grinning and make love to me," she said, squaring her shoulders, thrusting her breasts further in his face.

"Bossy, bossy, bossy."

He swept her into his arms and deposited her on the bed, enjoying her surprised 'oomph' as she stared up at him, tousled and blushing and absolutely ravishing.

"That's some move," she said, reaching up to trace his lips with her fingers, staring at him in wonderment as if she couldn't believe this was happening.

"I'll show you moves."

———

As Bo slid on top of her, Tahnee closed her eyes, giving herself over to the pleasure of exploring by touch. She ran her fingertips over the faint stubble darkening his jaw, over the soft cotton of his polo shirt, and lower to the expanse of firm skin where his shirt had ridden up. Lower still, to the waistband of his jeans where her fingers inveigled their way in but couldn't move further due to their position.

"You're wearing too many clothes," she grumbled, tugging impatiently at his button and zip, skimming her hand over the impressive bulge beneath.

"So are you."

He rolled off her and she opened her eyes, not wanting to miss this show. Though she'd seen most of Bo's body that morning, it would be nothing on a first-hand private showing up close and personal.

"You first."

"Okay." He whipped his polo shirt over his head and she sighed, running her hands over the firm planes of his chest and abdomen. He had a serious six-pack going on, the type of abs seen on elite athletes rather than authors and she vowed never to judge a book by its cover ever again.

"Want some help?" She tugged at his zipper, inching it down with an unsteady hand before slipping in to cup him, empowered by her boldness while heat scorched her cheeks.

His eyes closed, a tortured expression on his face. "If you want to see some of those moves I promised you, enough of that for now."

"What? No staying power?" She stroked his length once, twice, and chuckled as he growled and forcibly removed her hand from his open fly.

"I'll show you staying power."

He whipped off her skirt before she could blink and as he shimmied his way down her body, the determined glint in his eye set her pulse hammering in her veins.

For her, the build-up was everything and it looked like Bo was into foreplay as much as she was. However, when his mouth settled over her and he breathed on her, hot and heavy, she knew this would be no ordinary foreplay. Unlike the few times she'd had sex in the past, he was taking his time, not ripping off her underwear with the aim to satisfy his own desire. Bo had other ideas as he plucked at the elastic of her lace panties, his fingers skimming the skin underneath while his mouth continued to press against her most intimate spot.

Spirals warred with stars as they danced before her eyes, her vision blurring when he finally tugged her panties down and flicked her with his tongue in one glorious sweep.

"Oh yeah," she moaned, her legs falling open as he buried his head between them, licking her, stroking her wet folds, and sucking her until she almost passed out with the intensity of it.

As the ripples built and her body stiffened, he didn't let up, increasing the pace, flicking his tongue in circles, sucking her until she bucked and screamed his name.

"Wow," she muttered an eternity later, when the aftershocks had subsided and she lay limp against the damp sheets, stunned, stupefied and deliciously satisfied.

"You're beautiful," he said, joining her at the head of the bed again, stroking her hair back from her face and staring at her with such awe tears burned the back of her eyes.

"And you're very talented." She pulled his head down for a kiss, terrified she'd do something silly like cry if he continued to stare at her like that.

She kissed him with a hunger born of looking and not touching for too many days and she barely managed to stop devouring him by disengaging her lips and pointing to his legs.

"One of us is still overdressed."

He had his jeans and briefs off in one, smooth movement. "Not anymore."

Her heart hammered like a piston as she stared at his body, every glorious exposed inch of it; and several impressive inches in between.

He grinned at her blatant ogling and propped on an elbow in a classic centrefold pose. "See anything you like?"

"Don't fish for compliments. It's not very manly."

She forced herself to look away and try to act casual as if the sight of his tanned, hard body didn't do it for her.

"I'll show you manly." Slipping his arms around her, he rolled onto his back and pulled her with him until their bodies lay plastered skin to hot bare skin.

"I like being on top," she said, nuzzling his neck until he purred.

"I like you being there." He shifted his hips in a little mock thrust, showing her exactly how much.

"How about showing me some of those famous moves you were talking about earlier?" She wriggled on top of him, teasing.

"What did you think of the first one?"

"By the decibel of how loudly I shouted your name, I think you know."

Slanting his lips across hers, he probed her mouth with his tongue, daring her to meet him, to join him in another bone-melting kiss and she gave as good as she got, her bones liquefying with not much coercion at all.

"You want moves? How's this?" He yanked a bedside drawer opened, ripped open a foil packet and lifted her hips gently, sheathing himself while they both looked on; him with impatience, her with awe.

She was vigilant with protection but once again the guys she'd been with had made short work of it, fumbling and grumbling, while Bo made an art form of rolling it on.

"Not bad," she said, "but I've got a few moves of my own I'd like to show you."

"Be my guest."

His hands hovered on her hips as his eyes blazed a trail down her body, lingering where their bodies almost joined. Almost but not quite and she desperately wanted to change that.

With infinite slowness, she settled over his shaft and lowered herself, one exquisite inch at a time, watching his face contort with passion and desire, more empowered than she'd ever been in her life.

She did this to him. She turned him on, she gave him pleasure and once she'd taken him in fully and settled on top of him, she didn't want this feeling to end.

"You're so tight," he breathed, his hands wandering up her body to cup her breasts, his thumbs skimming her peaked nipples, sending ripples of excitement through her.

"Want to help me loosen up?"

He matched her smile and they stayed like that, grinning like a couple of goofballs as she started to slide up and down, taking the lead, setting the pace and revelling in the build-up all over again.

Tahnee didn't know how long she rode him but a fine sheen of sweat slicked their skins as their pace quickened to match their breathing, and as she contracted around him she gave herself over to the astounding pleasure of sex with the first guy to ever blow her mind.

"Tahnee..."

Her name tumbled from his lips in a guttural groan as he came, and as she collapsed on his chest and he cradled her tight, she fleetingly wondered how she could walk away from something this good.

TEN

*W*ally had walked around the muddy waterhole three times, two more laps than his usual daily waddle. He had a lot of energy today and he was tired of staying at home and digging. He needed some air. He needed a break from Kaz, who had cast some type of weird spell over him. She talked and laughed and smiled way too much. Now he had a headache.

Bo Bradford's blog.

"I can't believe you drove up here just for a coffee."

Tahnee tipped two sugars into her short black and stirred, more than a little grateful Carissa had showed up. She needed someone to talk to and chatting on the phone or sending texts didn't cut it for what she had to say.

"Come on, T, you know me better than that. I can get a great caramel latte back in Stockton. I'm here for the low-down." Carissa wiggled her eyebrows. "I want the first-hand, unabridged, unadulterated version, so spill."

"How's—"

"Stop." Carissa held up her hand. "You've asked about the kids, you've asked about Brody, you know Daisy is fine and my shop is doing a roaring trade. You can't possibly want to know about anyone else back home so how about you cut to the chase and put your poor, gossip-deprived sister out of her misery?"

"I was only going to ask how the plans for Brody's surprise party are coming along. Sheesh."

"Fine. Now, where were we?"

Tahnee chuckled at Carissa's fierce mock frown. "We were about to discuss my new job."

Carissa rolled her eyes. "I bet the new job is fine too. Besides, you're super talented and anyone can see it. How's *Bo*?"

Ah…the million dollar question. Bo was mighty fine: smart, good-looking, intelligent and an absolute tiger in bed. She'd never had it so good.

Then why the constant nagging doubt something wasn't right?

"Bo's incredible."

There, she'd admitted it to another person and the sky hadn't fallen in or lightning hadn't struck, though it looked like a bolt of Carissa's overenthusiastic advice could be just as bad.

"I knew it. Something's going on."

"Or something's coming off, depending on your point of view," Tahnee said, unable to keep the smug smile off her face.

"You trollop." Carissa grinned from ear to ear. "Details please."

Tahnee blushed just thinking about some of those 'details' and switched the conversation before she melted from the memories.

"Honestly? He's fabulous. We work together all day and it's magic. He's creative and demanding but I like that. I'm enjoying working with the author one on one for once rather than remotely, it gives me a new perspective on illustrating."

By the sly glint in Carissa's eyes, she knew what was coming before her sister opened her mouth. "And after work?"

"That's pretty magical too," Tahnee admitted, wondering how she could articulate how special Bo made her feel and knowing she'd come up empty no matter how hard she tried. "I've never met anyone like him before."

"Wow, it sounds serious." Concern replaced the cheeky gleam in Carissa's eyes.

"It's not."

Far from it; Tahnee had made that perfectly clear when she'd accepted the ground rules he'd laid out earlier in the week, and of course he'd only been too happy to go along. What guy wouldn't? With her offering commitment-free sex as an added bonus to her stay, he probably thought all his Christmas's and birthdays had come at once.

It should've been the perfect situation for them though somehow, the more time they spent together, the more she wondered if she'd made a terrible mistake. Not in sleeping with Bo—she'd never regret the magic they created in bed—but the expiry date stipulation to their fling had her surprisingly angsty.

Why should something this great end so soon? It wasn't like she expected a family and white picket fence tomorrow. She could have some serious fun with Bo, could explore and develop what they had and who knew, maybe an anti-social guy could change?

"You're in love with him," Carissa said softly, her eyes wide with surprise.

Tahnee absorbed the shock of hearing the possibility of

her losing her mind verbalised and took several gulps of scalding coffee before replying. "You can't fall for someone in a week."

"Really? I fell for Brody in about that time."

Tahnee snorted. "You two took months to sort out your relationship."

"And whose fault was that?" Carissa absentmindedly stirred her coffee, a goofy expression on her face. "I knew he was the one the minute I saw him frowning at me from over the fence. Not my fault he took longer to come to his senses."

"That's not the point. We're not talking about love here. I like the guy, that's all."

"You sure there's not more to it?"

"Of course I'm not sure," she snapped, immediately regretting her outburst and mouthing "sorry" to her sister.

"Look at me, I'm a mess. I don't know what to wear in the mornings any more, I actually wear lipgloss every day and I find myself doodling. Me. The queen of anti-doodlers."

The corners of Carissa's mouth twitched and she quickly lifted her mug to conceal her smile. "As long as it's not initials in hearts, doodling is perfectly normal."

"No it's not. It's crazy behaviour." Tahnee made circles at her temple. "It's the warped, twisted behaviour of someone in...like," she finished lamely, unable to contemplate she could've fallen in love with Bo let alone say it.

Carissa reached across the table and squeezed her hand. "Listen up. This is the best advice you're ever going to get on the love issue. You don't choose to fall in love, it happens. You don't pick the guy, he comes along one day and suddenly he's there and you can't imagine not being with him." She squeezed again. "Love isn't about hearts and flowers and romantic dinners. It's about following your instinct and acknowledging a feeling deep down that your life wouldn't be the same without that guy in it. Is that what you feel for Bo?"

Tahnee closed her eyes and tried to picture her life without Bo. The churning in her stomach intensified and her chest ached. Surely she hadn't fallen for him?

"You'll be fine, trust your instincts." Carissa squeezed her hand once more before releasing it and Tahnee opened her eyes, mustering the nastiest glare she could summon. "Hey, don't shoot the messenger. I'm only trying to help."

Tahnee slumped, unwelcome tears stinging her eyes. "I know. It just wasn't supposed to happen like this."

It wasn't supposed to happen at all. No matter how perfect Bo appeared, he wasn't the right guy for her. He'd virtually said as much yet she'd gone ahead and fallen for him anyway.

How stupid could she be?

"Go with the flow, okay?"

She mustered a wan smile for her sister. Go with the flow? This should be interesting.

Her cell rang and she slid it out of her handbag. "Tahnee speaking."

"Hey, it's Bo."

His low, gravelly voice did something to her insides as heat spread through her body like molten honey.

"Hi. What's up?"

"Are you free tonight?"

"Yeah, sure."

She could've played it a little cooler, maybe drawn out her response, pretended to check her diary. But hot on the realisation she may actually feel something for him, what was the point?

"Great. I have a surprise for you. Maybe we can go down to the The Rocks, have that coffee we didn't get around to after the awards night ,and I'll spring the surprise later? What do you think?"

She thought it sounded like the best offer she'd had in

ages. Apart from the naughty one he'd already made, the same one that her melting at the sound of his low voice.

"Sounds great. Thanks for asking."

"No problem. Just thought I'd let you know well in advance."

She smiled. He really was a thoughtful guy. "Why? The shock of this surprise isn't going to kill me, is it?"

He hesitated and she imagined him sitting behind his desk, that tiny crease between his brows as he pondered her question. She adored that little crease; it made him look so studious, so focussed.

"I certainly hope not. I've gotten used to having you around."

Her heart tripped at the implied meaning behind his words. Was he simply making a statement or did he like being with her as much as she loved being with him?

"Great," she said, wanting to lean forward and thump her head on the table for such a lame response.

Why couldn't she have said 'I like being with you too' or something similar? Then again, she was an illustrator. He had the fancy way with words.

His deep chuckles washed over her and she shivered despite the warm sunshine filtering through an umbrella shade. "I'll see you later then?"

She didn't know what prompted her to lower her tone and almost purr into the phone. "You sure will."

"Hurry." One simple word filled with promise and need and heat.

She hung up, sat back and picked up a serviette to fan her face.

"I don't need to ask who that was," Carissa said, smirking before she drained her coffee and reached for her purse.

"He has a surprise for me."

"I bet he does by your neon pink cheeks."

Tahnee's hands flew to her cheeks and she covered them with cool palms. "Promise you won't breathe a word of how pathetic I am to anybody?"

"Promise," Carissa chuckled. "Now, I must run. Daisy can only mind Jack until three so you have fun with your sexy author, okay?"

"I'll try." Tahnee pulled a face, already wondering what the surprise could be, hoping it wasn't her marching orders.

"Relax, T. Everything's going to be fine, you'll see."

Tahnee returned Carissa's fierce hug, hoping her sister was right.

"How's the book coming along?"

Bo glared at Tahnee while she propped on the corner of his desk, her leg swinging provocatively and grabbing his attention from the PC screen.

"Right on track if a certain sexy illustrator would stop trying to distract me and get back to her work."

"I will if you give me a hint what the surprise is."

Bo shook his head and made a zipping motion with his hand over his lips.

"Come on, just one, tiny clue." She picked up Wally and Kaz and contorted them into sexual positions, laughing when he grabbed them out of her hand and rearranged them in a platonic configuration.

"No. Quit bugging me."

"You sound awfully tense. Something on your mind?" Her deliberately husky voice had him sitting bolt upright.

"The only thing on my mind is writing words about these fellas," he said, his mouth twitching with amusement as she inched her foot closer to him with the aim to play footsies, though with an appendage a tad higher. "The book's running ahead of schedule and I'd like to keep it that way."

He guided her foot away just as she'd been about to reach the good stuff. "You're not sticking to the rules. No play during work hours, remember?"

She pretended to pout, and his eyes focussed on her mouth as she'd intended. "But you told me to hurry back over the phone. And you're a tease, dangling this surprise in front of me then making me wait until tonight."

"But anticipation is half the fun," he said, his hand shooting out and capturing her leg, giving it a gentle tug until she tumbled into his lap. "Don't you think?"

She wriggled, and by the flare of excitement in her eyes she revelled in her power as a woman as she encountered the hard evidence of how much he wanted her nestled snugly against her butt.

"I think you enjoy keeping me on the edge."

"Too right," he said, trailing his forefinger down her cheek, across her lips and lower, brushing the top of her breasts with the barest of touches. "But for now, we must work. Otherwise no play later and I know how much you want me."

"Ha. Shows how much you know." She bounded out of his lap and sent a pointed glance at his groin. "It's the other way around. You want me. *Real* bad."

They laughed in unison before she strutted across the room to her resident couch, and he knew he had as much chance of getting any work done for the rest of the afternoon as he had of forgetting her once the two weeks were up.

Absolutely none.

"It's worth it, you'll see," he said, as she glared at him, unable to sustain her mock anger when she smiled, and all she could think was how much he wanted her to come back to his desk and straddle him again.

"It better be," she said, picking up her sketchpad and raising it as a barrier between them, trying to block out his deep chuckles.

He couldn't wait for tonight.

Eleven

After sharing a quiet drink with Kaz down by the waterhole, Wally didn't feel so good. Sure, he liked Kaz, but she asked too many questions and wanted to talk all the time. Sometimes, a wombat just wanted to be on his own. Why couldn't a kangaroo understand that? He had to tell her. But what if he hurt her feelings? Boy, making a new friend was tough.

Bo Bradford's blog.

Sipping her coffee, Tahnee tried not to stare at Bo. No mean feat considering the guy looked like a fantasy dream date in his black polo and dark denim. She'd been practically drooling over him all night, her gaze riveted to his face while they chatted, trying to stay focussed on what he was saying while her mind repeatedly drifted to the magic he wielded with those lips. The guy was bad for her concentration and in a trendy café filled with cute guys, he stood out.

"You're inhaling that coffee."

Her gaze snapped to his, amusement highlighting the

golden flecks in a sea of green. She'd never seen anyone with green eyes before, not the intense colour of Bo's, and their unique colour had her staring more than usual. Her excuse, she was sticking to it.

"It's good coffee," she said, sending him her best flirty glance over the rim of the tall glass. "Lucky you made it a double."

"I'm not surprised you're up all night with the amount of caffeine you drink."

She saw the second his words registered, a slow, sexy smile spreading across his face as he recalled exactly what kept them up at night.

"I haven't heard you complaining," she said, setting her glass on the table and folding her arms, knowing the simple action would press her breasts together and act as an instant cleavage enhancer. A slick move she'd seen on some rom-com movie to capture a guy's attention and by the widening of Bo's eyes, it worked.

"I'm not," he said, tearing his gaze away from her cleavage to shake his head. "I know what you're up to, trying to distract me and get me home so you can have your way with me."

Chuckling, she said, "You got me. Is my cheap and tawdry ploy working?"

"Oh yeah, it's working all right." His voice lowered, the husky timbre sending a thrill of anticipation through her. "I'm trying really hard not to be a chauvinistic pig and keep my gaze fixed on your chest but you're making it damn difficult."

Thrilled with their banter, she leaned forward and did a little shimmy. "What? These things? Nothing you haven't seen before."

She could tease him all night, resurrecting memories of how many times he'd seen her bare breasts, not to mention her naked body. Of how many times he'd kissed and licked his way over every inch of her skin, coming back for seconds like a man starved. But then she'd be doing herself a disservice considering every time she teased him and elicited a response, desire flowed through her body, hot, swift and all-consuming.

"You're a bad girl." By his appreciative expression, he loved it.

"You bring out that side of me."

None of the other guys she'd dated had made her feel so wanton, so carefree, like she could say anything and do anything. Then again, none of those guys had turned her on like Bo and she couldn't afford to like him so damn much, not when they had an expiration date.

"What's with the serious face?" He reached across the table and captured her hand, his touch never failing to make her feel cherished and secure, two feelings she'd craved her whole life.

Her foster parents had gone a long way to alleviating her insecurities but her inadequacies never quite left her, the early childhood years of being forcibly separated from her sisters a lasting nightmarish imprint on her soul.

Stan had been a lot like Bo actually, a quiet man who valued his privacy, who wasn't overly talkative at the best of times. In a way, Stan's reticence hadn't allayed her fear she could lose her new parents and get kicked out on the street at any time. She'd loved him, but maybe if he'd been more demonstrative, more verbose with his emotions, she mightn't still be hung up over stability and needing to belong?

"Just thinking about old memories," she said, annoyed she could think badly of Stan. Along with Doris, her foster parents had done their best in raising her. They'd loved her, even if they hadn't been overly affectionate.

His hand slackened its grip. "You're thinking about another guy?"

Rolling her eyes, she said, "Your ego is safe for now. I was actually thinking about how nice this is, being here with you, holding hands. It makes me feel good."

His rueful smile reached his eyes. "But what's that got to do with old memories?"

Tahnee paused, wondering how much she should tell him. She'd been upfront with him until now, not wasting time hedging when they had so little time together. But was it too soon to talk about the possibility of an ongoing relationship beyond two weeks? Was it time to change the rules?

Not wanting to spoil this evening—or her surprise—she decided to hold off on opening up completely. After all, they had time.

The rest of their lives if she had any say in it.

She settled for telling him a partial truth. "Feeling good in the moment brings up other good memories. You know the type of thing. Getting your first bike, baking cookies with your mum, waking up on Christmas morning. That's all I was thinking about, family stuff."

If she'd thrown a bucket of iced water over Bo, it would've had a similar reaction. His face froze, his eyes dimmed and he slipped his hand away on the pretext of grabbing his coffee. Lame, considering he had all but dregs left in his cup.

"Actually, I don't know," he said, gripping the cup like a life buoy. "I guess you got to play happy families growing up, I didn't."

If he only knew. "Want to talk about it?"

"Not much to tell."

His harsh laugh saddened her as much as his expressionless face. Maybe if he opened up about his family, she'd have more chance of understanding him and in turn, of getting closer to him?

If they wanted to take their relationship to the next level, surely they needed to trust each other enough to talk about their pasts? She'd expect nothing less from her partner and as she watched Bo, frozen in his pensive silence, the first sliver of doubt sent a shiver of foreboding down her spine.

What if Bo was emotionally shut off, the type of guy who couldn't or wouldn't articulate his feelings? A guy like Stan? She couldn't live her life with that type of uncertainty again. If she'd learned one thing growing up, it was to look out for herself, to not rely on other people.

Easier said than done and right now, she needed Bo to wrap his arms around her and tell her everything would be okay. Instead, he sat there, immobile, moody, closed off, and her heart gave a shudder.

"Surely you can tell me something your family?"

A deep groove slashed his brows, formidable and disapproving. "My folks were all about keeping up appearances in society, hell-bent on schmoozing as much as possible. They loved Brennan and me but we didn't get to see them much. Guess I hold a grudge for that. Then when Mum died, I thought 'what a waste'."

"But you hang out with your dad and Brennan, right?"

He nodded, some of the tension leaving him. "Yeah. We're good buddies, even if I'm not in their boys' club anymore. My dad's cool for an uptight banker and Brennan is a party boy who never grew up."

"You could've been like them," she said, resisting the urge to slap a hand across her mouth when she realised she'd spoken out loud.

He smiled, his stare appreciative. "Yeah, but I'm not, thank goodness. You really speak your mind, don't you?"

She nodded, glad he found it endearing rather than a pain as most guys usually did. "What's the point of avoidance? Better to face things head-on."

Like telling Bo how she felt.

Like telling him how much she wanted to give them a chance beyond next week.

Like telling him he was the best thing that had ever happened to her.

Thankfully, he stood, grabbed her hand and tugged her towards the door.

"Hey, if this caveman act is your idea of providing an evening's entertainment, I'd like to see what you do for an encore."

"I'll show you when we get back to my place," he said, holding open the door for her, his smouldering stare leaving her in little doubt he would follow up on his bold promise.

"What about my surprise?"

"Soon," he said, his lips brushing hers for an exquisite, prolonged moment before he pulled away. "Very soon."

———

Bo remained silent on the drive home, deep in thought, pondering the trance Tahnee had him in most of the time. He was drawn to her like kids to his books; a phenomenon he couldn't explain but was amazed by just the same.

"You're in a hurry."

Glancing down at the speedometer, he eased his foot off the accelerator and slowed as the traffic light ahead turned red. "Sorry. Mind on other things."

"I bet," she said in a sultry voice reminiscent of his favourite jazz singer. "Looking forward to getting home, huh?"

Warning bells clanged in his head. For some inexplicable reason, her slip of the tongue in saying 'home' implying it was hers too made him wonder if she thought there was more to their relationship than stipulated. He'd been clear on the ground rules and she'd been more than happy to stick to them.

No commitment. No envisioning a future beyond two weeks. The perfect situation for both of them.

But something in the way 'home' rolled off her tongue cued him in that maybe, just maybe, the rules had changed. And that scared the hell out of him.

"Yeah, I'm a homebody and I always look forward to returning after I've been out." He played it cool, not wanting to jump to any conclusions, but once his anti-commitment antenna had gone up, he was having a difficult time switching off his mental alarm.

"Me too." She paused, studying his face with an intensity that made him squirm. "Is something wrong?"

Plenty, if he listened to his gut, the same instinct that had woken him up to the foibles of the financial world. His instinct had served him well in the past and he'd be damned if he ignored it now and right at this minute, it was telling him Tahnee wanted more from him than he could give.

Forcing a smile, he said, "No, I'm fine. Probably shell-shocked from being surrounded by so many people at that café. You know I don't get out often."

Visiting trendy spots like the café he'd chosen tonight because he thought she'd like it reminded him too much of his financier days, when winning over the customer and coming out on top were the primary objectives, people and job satisfaction be damned. No surprise he'd traded his portfolio for a healthy dose of imagination.

Her puzzled frown didn't detract from her beauty one iota. On any other woman, a frown would've added unattractive wrinkles to her forehead. On Tahnee, a few lines made her cuter.

"You really are a hermit, aren't you?"

"Yeah, and proud of it."

Dealing with a bunch of fictional animal characters was a hell of a lot better than dealing with a bunch of money-oriented fakers on a daily basis.

Her frown didn't disappear. If anything, it intensified after his answer. "I'm surprised a guy your age isn't out partying and whooping it up."

"A guy my age?"

She rolled her eyes. "Don't go fishing for compliments. What are you, mid-thirties max?"

"Thirty-four."

She snapped her fingers. "There you go. Why aren't you out there using your fame to pick up women and impress the heck out of everyone else? I don't get it."

Bo didn't like questions, especially the probing questions Tahnee fired at him with both barrels. *This* was why he lived like a recluse. Why delve when he knew the reasons behind his withdrawing from society weren't all that exciting? He'd had enough of the rat-race and wanted to set his own pace. Not particularly riveting.

Though he'd hazard a guess she'd find his secret identity interesting. Not that she'd ever find out. Nobody would, just the way he'd intended when he hid away in his mansion five years ago.

He shrugged, not wanting to give her a sniff of how he hated this type of interrogation. "There's nothing to understand. I value my privacy. Authors are renowned for liking their own company, which is how they manage to keep their butts planted in chairs long enough to churn out books and meet deadlines. No big secret."

She knew he was fobbing her off. He could see it in the quirk of her eyebrow, in the 'I'm not impressed' compression of her lips, and the steady, unwavering stare.

Damn, what had happened to flirting over coffee, offering her a great job—his surprise they hadn't got around to yet—and heading back to his place for more mind-blowing sex?

"I guess not," she finally said. "Seeing as I'm willing to let you off the hook, how about you get this car moving? Particularly since the light has been green for the last minute."

Muttering an exasperated, "Thanks for the heads-up," he turned left at the next intersection and headed for home.

"Race you to the bedroom when we get there?" Her soft question rose over the filtered jazz filling the car and he sped up.

"You're on," he said, hoping by the time she discovered her surprise, they weren't off.

―――

Bo drove like a maniac, covering the distance between The Rocks and Rose Bay in record time. He drove like he had a demon on his tail, but Tahnee didn't mind. It added to the thrill, the rush of being with a guy who did it for her in every way.

After stopping the car with a spray of gravel in front of the mansion, he ran around the car, opened her door and helped her out.

"You're in an awful hurry to get inside," she said, raising on tip-toes to press her lips to his, unable to wait a second longer for that first, magical rush when they kissed.

"I want you so badly," he said, pulling her into his arms, burying his face in her hair, and she sighed, inhaling the heady combination of spice and oak, the scent that lingered on his pillows, the scent that would linger in her memory long after she'd left.

If she left.

"Hmm...I can feel how much." She wriggled her hips, inflaming his desire, making his erection twitch with reflex eagerness.

Straightening, he captured her chin in his hand and tilted her face up so he could stare into her eyes, and she wondered if he could read the need in hers. He didn't blink, he didn't speak, his fingers lightly caressing her cheek while his intense stare bored into her, compelling her to understand something she had no idea about.

"You okay?"

"Come inside and I'll show you how much," he said, dropping a soft, lingering kiss on her lips before leading her up the front steps and into the house.

"You've been awfully quiet," she said, slipping off her stilettos as the door shut, her sudden loss of height making her feel petite and in need of a strong man to carry her upstairs and have his way with her.

"I'd rather be doing this than talking."

Her breath left her lungs in a whoosh as he plastered his mouth to hers, coaxing a response with the barest flick of his tongue. Her lips parted beneath his and he deepened the kiss, ravaging her mouth with pent-up desire and a wealth of skill she'd come to expect from their sensational love-making.

"Wow," she murmured, her head falling back to expose her neck to him, a highly erogenous zone by past experience of the last week, and he kissed his way down to her breasts, nipping at her cleavage, sending shards of delight through her body.

Recapturing her mouth, he crushed his lips to hers in a hot, open-mouthed, smouldering kiss that left her weak and clinging to him.

She sensed this wasn't a night for long, slow seductions. They'd been dancing around each other all day with subtle glances while working, playing word games designed to entice and prolong the desire that grew between them with every passing second.

She needed him, right here, right now; his hands all over her, skimming the bare flesh on her back, cupping her butt, squeezing her against him.

"We're not going to make it to the bedroom, are we?"

She didn't answer his question. Instead, her hands slipped to his fly and she had him unzipped and out in a second. He groaned and backed her against the nearest wall, pressing his mouth to hers in a blistering kiss, the type of kiss a prelude to lose-your-mind-blow-the-consequences type of sex, as he fumbled in his wallet and sheathed himself in the time it took for her to untie the knot holding her halter top up.

"Bo, oh yeah," she gasped as he caressed her breasts, kneading them, cupping their fullness while flicking his thumb against her nipples.

Her heartbeat throbbed in her ears as she arched against him, his hands dropping to her skirt, bunching the cotton folds and yanking upward until his erection nudged her.

He rubbed himself against her, once, twice, her low moan all the incentive he needed to rip the scrap of lace off her and nudge toward her slick entrance.

"This is going to be hard and fast," he murmured, tearing his polo over his head, pressing against her, hot hard chest plastered to her searing skin as waves of unparalleled sensation rippled through her.

She desperately needed more of him, her hunger fuelled by a mind-numbing lust she'd never anticipated in her wildest dreams, and an overwhelming urgency to lose herself in the moment.

She'd never had sex like this before, the type of frantic sex romance novels depicted but were pure fiction as far as she was concerned, and with a talented partner like Bo she knew this encounter would far surpass any words generated on paper.

"Hard and fast is good," she said, hooking her leg around his waist and pushing against him, her wet folds surrounding the tip of him before he knew what was happening.

"Tahnee," he breathed, burying himself in her to the hilt, filling her as she gasped in ecstasy, transporting her as he withdrew and repeated the action, pumping into her with a speed designed for pleasure and ultimate satisfaction.

Her breathy moans fired him and he grabbed her butt,

hoisted her up and held her against the wall as she wrapped her legs around him, effectively imprisoning him deep within her.

In and out, faster...faster...the friction building to a climax that threatened to shoot her into orbit and explode into a million stars. She'd never felt like this, so totally connected to a guy, and as her hips ground against his, her mouth open and eager beneath his and she groaned her climax in a primitive sound totally alien for her, she knew it would be damn near impossible to leave him at the end of the week if that's what he still wanted.

Savouring their emotional connection almost as much as the physical, she squeezed him tighter as he surged toward climax, the pressure rebuilding in heart-stopping waves as he pounded into her, obliterating everything but this moment, this man, and the ecstasy they created as he came along with her.

"Wow," she said, resting her head against the wall, sweat covering her face and her exposed breasts, her nipples thrusting toward him in hard peaks.

She should've been self-conscious but wasn't. What was left to hide from the man who'd connected with her on so many levels, who'd taken her to heaven and back and who could keep her there if only he felt as much for her as she did for him?

"You okay?"

"Never better." She smiled, the smug smile of a satisfied woman and he grinned in return, making her feel like she'd given him the best gift and he hadn't been disappointed when he'd ripped off the wrapping.

"Want to take a shower?" He kissed her taut nipples and the sparks flared in an instant, the embers of their slaked passion needing little to re-combust.

"You're full of good ideas," she said, burying her face in his neck, savouring the closeness, wrapped around him as he carried her to the bathroom.

Wishing she could stay this close to him forever.

Tahnee had died and gone to heaven.

She'd read somewhere that orgasms were like little deaths and if so, she'd curled up her toes three times during the night...and how.

Rolling onto her side slowly so wouldn't wake Bo, she snuggled under the duvet, content to watch him sleep. Early morning sunlight filtered through the wooden blinds, bathing him in a diffuse, ethereal light. She'd never seen anything so beautiful as this incredible man deep in slumber, his long eyelashes casting spiky shadows on his cheeks, his perfect mouth slightly tilted at the corners, his usually animated face so relaxed and peaceful. As for the rest of him...he really was beautiful.

"Good morning."

Her gaze drifted up from admiring the sculpted planes of his chest to meet his eyes, half-hooded and watching her with clear intent. "Hey there, sleepyhead."

She brushed her lips across his, not caring about morning breath or bed hair or anything inconsequential. She was right where she wanted to be, waking up next to the sexiest guy in the world.

"Are you thinking what I'm thinking?"

"What are you thinking?" She snuggled closer, not requiring any mind-reading skills. She'd seen the glint in his eyes and could feel the hard evidence prodding her stomach. "Oh, *that*. Not much thinking going on there, unless it's true what they say about guys, that their brains are located in their—"

"Hey, I've just woken up. Leave the insults for later, at least until we start work. You do realise it's Monday morning?"

Just like that, her libido wilted as she realised this was their last week together and she hadn't got around to broaching the subject of what happened at the end of it. Her intentions to talk had fallen by the wayside somewhere between a sensational short black during their date and barely making it through the front door before having the kind of sex that made a girl forget everything but her name.

"Don't remind me," she said, rolling onto her back and flinging her forearm across her eyes. "My boss is a slavedriver and he won't understand if I'm late because I was distracted having sensational sex with an amazing guy."

He tugged her forearm away, a huge grin on his face. "You think I'm amazing?"

And more. Despite his anti-social quirks, Bo was one heck of a guy and she'd fallen for him in less time than it took her to decide what colour to paint her armoire.

Rolling her eyes in mock exasperation, she said, "Don't let it go to your head."

He glanced down at his erection, smug and proud. "Too late for that."

"You're such a guy." She rolled onto her side and curled into him, squealing when he started tickling her, wishing this could go on forever. Maybe it could if she ever got around to broaching the subject.

"Before we get too carried away, how about that surprise I mentioned yesterday?"

She slapped her forehead. "I can't believe I forgot in all the excitement."

They grinned, the smug, satisfied smiles of two people who had got caught up in the 'excitement' several times last night.

"Is it in this room?" She looked around while he covered her hands with his, plastering them against his hard chest, his heart thumping steadily beneath her palms as she wondered if he felt half as much for her as she did for him.

"You could say that," he said, staring into her eyes with the type of intent that had her conjuring up all sorts of wonderful dreams, particularly the best dream of all, the forever one.

"How about we extend our arrangement beyond the end of this week?"

Her heart stopped for a breath-taking moment before racing at a million beats a minute.

"Are you serious?" She almost whispered, too afraid to speak louder in case she'd spoil the magical aura surrounding them. Bo had just uttered the words she'd hoped for and she couldn't believe it.

Laughing at her stunned expression, he said, "Of course I'm serious. Surely you know you're the best illustrator in the business and I'd be a fool to let you go."

Illustrator...best in the business...fool...

The words were sharp pins stabbing at her bubble of happiness until she had nothing left but a deflated empty balloon of devastation.

One word stuck in her consciousness: fool.

Bo hadn't been the fool, she had, for forgetting his damn rules and losing her heart in the process.

"You're talking about extending my contract?"

"Of course. Just because you won't be here doesn't mean we can't work together remotely. You already told me you worked from home for other authors, we can do the same. Great surprise, huh? What do you say?"

She wanted to say he was crazy if he thought for one second she'd put herself through that. Stupidly, she'd harboured the faintest hope maybe she'd got his initial offer wrong, that maybe he wanted her to stay around? However, he'd made it clear: he was offering her a job, nothing else. She would return to Stockton, he'd stay here, and they would make one, big, happy book together. Several books if they were lucky.

"I need some time to think about it."

Time to get her emotions under control before she started blubbering like the deluded fool she was. Time to get away from his potent presence and think about what refusing him could do to her career and ultimately her dream of owning her own home and a piece of lifetime security. Most of all, time to mend her shattered heart.

His grip on her hands slackened and she used the opportunity to slip hers away on the pretext of twisting her messy hair into a top knot, when in reality she couldn't bear to feel his heart pounding beneath her palms, the heart she would never have.

He frowned. "You don't sound so thrilled."

"It's not that—" She clamped her lips shut, wishing she had the sense to keep her mouth closed for once. In this case, her usual bluntness wouldn't be an asset and predictably, he pounced.

"Then what's up? I thought you'd want to continue our arrangement beyond the two weeks."

Tahnee tried not to wince. It was the second time he'd called what they shared an 'arrangement' and she hated it. Then again, what did she expect? He'd laid out the rules, she followed them. End of story.

But she didn't want their story to end, not at the conclusion of the week, not ever. She wanted the story to turn into a fairytale, with her and the greatest guy she'd ever met in starring roles.

Like that was going to happen.

In that moment, awareness flared in his eyes and his lips thinned into a hard line.

He knew.

Damn it, he'd twigged, and she searched her brain for a quick way to throw him off track, to pretend like she was fine with his offer, was fine with ending their relationship at the end of the week.

For that's exactly what this was, a relationship, not an *arrangement*. Bo could call it whatever he liked, could dress it up or dress it down, but they'd had more than a casual fling no matter what he thought or how callously he described it.

"This isn't about my job offer, is it?" His stricken expression implied he wasn't too thrilled by the idea her reaction could mean something more.

Sighing, she said, "No."

"You agreed to the rules. What's changed?"

With razor-sharp precision, he zeroed in on what was bothering her. She should've been glad he was so tuned in to her feelings and had the guts to confront her rather than dance around the main issue like most guys would've. However, how could she be glad when his eyes had hardened to a flinty green?

For an awful moment, her lower lip quivered. She couldn't cry. She wouldn't, but as the realisation sunk in that he didn't want to have this conversation let alone anything more to do with her, her eyes stung.

He didn't reach across to her. He didn't caress her cheek with tenderness like he usually did or trace her lips like he'd never seen them before. He didn't smile or wink or broach the distance between them that yawned across the bed as wide as the Simpson Desert. He didn't do anything but stare at her with cool calculation as if trying to gauge her mood and she took a deep breath, hating herself for putting herself in this position.

"Maybe I've changed," she said, plucking at the sheet laying crumpled beneath them, a stark reminder of how many times it had twisted around them last night. "Maybe always following rules isn't fun."

He didn't smile. "Rules are made to protect people and in this case they were important. We didn't want to screw up our work, remember?"

An ache blossomed in her heart as she realised that work was his major concern. Not her or her feelings but the fact he might not get his precious pictures finished if she turned into a woman scorned. Jeez, didn't he give her any credit?

"This has nothing to do with work." They had to have this conversation, one way or another. "This is about you and me and you know it."

If his expression grew any bleaker, his face would freeze. "I thought you were happy sticking to the rules. I didn't think you wanted more?"

"I've changed my mind."

There, she'd said it, virtually admitting she was putty in his capable hands.

He shook his head, running a hand through his mussed hair. "I can't give you what you want."

His muttered words chilled her to the bone and she tugged the duvet higher, wishing she could snuggle into its warmth, pull it over her head and not come out until the rest of this week was over.

He couldn't give her what she wanted? He'd got that right. She wanted a guy to love her, to cherish her, to create a happy home with, to make babies with, to fill that home with warmth and laughter and all the good things in life.

Most of all, she wanted rock-solid stability, something she'd never been certain of growing up. She wanted her guy to give her all that and more and by Bo's cold reaction, he wasn't that guy.

She could've let him off the hook but a small part of her wanted to make him squirm. "What do you think I want?"

Pushing into a sitting position, she clutched the duvet around her like a protective shield, hating how vulnerable she felt.

"Don't do this, Tahnee."

"Do what? Be honest about how I feel?" She snapped her fingers, hoping her temper wouldn't follow suit. "That's right. Honesty about feelings takes guts and I guess you wouldn't get that, the way you hide away all the time to avoid confrontation."

"This is exactly what I didn't want to happen." He rolled away from her and out of bed, tugging on a pair of black boxers, but not before she had a mouth-watering eyeful of the best butt this side of the Pacific.

Not fair. He shouldn't be distracting her when they were about to have their first proper fight. Maybe they were headed for a relationship after all?

"I didn't expect this either," she said, relieved when he didn't walk out on her, wishing he'd pull a shirt over his head to keep her from staring at his broad chest, the same chest she'd licked and kissed and tickled so many times over the last week. "And I'm not expecting anything from you. I just thought...when you said..." she trailed off, hating the distance between them, hating his defensive posture, folded arms over his chest.

"I like you. I've had a great time this last week and we work really well together. By extending your contract, I thought you'd know how much I appreciate your talent, but as for anything else..." he shook his head, having the decency to look sad. "I'm better off alone, let's leave it at that."

"Let's," she snapped, bundling the duvet around her as she struggled to her feet, desperate to get out of the room before she bawled.

Head high, she stalked toward the door, trying to look as

elegant as possible considering she had a bulky burgundy and black striped duvet wrapped around her.

"I'm sorry," he said, his tone soft and dejected.

She didn't look back as she slammed the door on her way out.

Twelve

Wally dug harder. His claws scrabbled in the dirt, faster than ever before. Work was good. It kept his mind off other things, like the fight he'd had with Kaz. Wally didn't like it. Kaz had become his new best friend so why did she have to make things so hard? He liked his own burrow. He didn't want her to move in. Why couldn't she understand a wombat needed space?

Bo Bradford's blog.

Bo stared at the blank computer screen, his fingers poised over the keyboard. He willed the words to come and when they didn't, cursed his stubbornly silent muse. Anger made him want to thump the keyboard when he realised he had his first full-blown case of writer's block.

It had never happened to him before. He didn't believe in it. He preferred to think if he sat in his chair every day and made himself write he couldn't get blocked. Even if the work wasn't great, getting something down on the page was better than nothing. He could fix crap, he couldn't fix a blank page.

However, the longer he stared at the screen and the higher his blood pressure rose, he knew something had to give and it sure as hell wasn't his productivity.

Pushing away from the desk, he grabbed his laptop case from underneath it. Maybe he needed a fresh environment, somewhere to stimulate his creativity away from the mundane routine of his office?

He shovelled writing pads and pens into his case, studiously avoiding looking at the couch opposite and the usual place he found his creative stimulus.

Not that Tahnee would've noticed if he jumped up on his desk and started doing the Macarena. She'd been just as careful to avoid glancing his way for the last half hour, her head bent over her sketchpad until he wondered if she'd fallen asleep.

He had to survive another four days of this; four whole days of awkward greetings, frigid silences, and a sinking feeling this entire fiasco was his fault.

Waking up next to her yesterday morning had been great. It had been the aftermath of their little conversation when he'd sprung his surprise on her that had shattered their friendship beyond repair. He'd decided to give her space and gone out for the day.

'Give her space' could be construed that he was too chicken to face any more deep and meaningful revelations but it had done the trick. They hadn't seen each other all day and he'd half expected her to have vanished by the time he got back yet here she was, reporting for duty the day after, looking incredibly sexy in yet another pair of tight denim jeans, a pink fitted T-shirt hugging the breasts he couldn't get enough of and her shiny blonde hair loose around her shoulders, effectively screening her face from his curious glance.

And he was curious. He wanted to see her face, read her eyes, get a feel for where she was at with what he hoped was a hiccup to their working relationship. Not that he was being intentionally callous but he couldn't think beyond work, couldn't entertain the thought of having a full-blown relationship with someone who didn't know who he really was let alone inflict his grouchy personality on another human longterm, especially someone as special as her.

"If you're going to stand there all day and watch me, I'd rather work elsewhere." She raised her head and glared at him, her blue eyes frosty.

Yep, he could get a reading now clear as day and the message read: eff off.

"I was just leaving," he said, picking up his laptop case and hoisting the strap over his shoulder. "Thought I'd work offsite today."

She knew he was running away by the derisive curl of her lips. "You only have two more scenes to write and then we're done, right?"

He nodded, surprised by how much he hated hearing the truth. What if she didn't accept his offer? What if the way he'd bungled his way through her revelation of wanting more had driven an irreversible wedge between them?

"Two scenes, and that's it, Bo?" She prompted.

Refocussing, he said, "Yeah. You're so quick, we should be finished ahead of schedule."

She bent her head again, her hair shielding her face. "Good."

That was it. One word uttered in a voice devoid of inflection or emotion so he had no idea if she meant she was pleased about meeting the deadline or she couldn't wait to get the hell out of here. And the worst part? He didn't want to push her for an answer.

"I'll see you later," he said, heading for the door, hating her grunted response, hating how it had come to this more.

Tahnee stayed frozen until she heard the front door slam and Bo's car rev before unfolding her stiff legs from the sofa and padding across to the window, her bare feet enjoying the cold bite of the floorboards.

Her entire body ached from holding herself rigid for the last half hour, ever since he'd walked into the office and mumbled a greeting. She'd forced herself not to look up, not to move, to stay focussed on her work. It was the only way she could not break down, snap a pencil, or throw her entire box of charcoals at him.

Watching him race down the gravel drive and out of the fancy wrought-iron front gate like he had the devil chasing him, she flipped him the finger.

Bo was running scared.

He'd avoided her yesterday and now it looked like more of the same. Shaking her head, she turned away from the window and plopped onto the couch, swinging her feet up and lying back with her head resting in her hands.

She'd contemplated confronting him again but knew it wouldn't do any good. She'd tried to be honest and look where it had got her? On the verge of walking away from the best job opportunity ever and all because she'd been stupid enough to fall in love with the boss.

Cringing, she pummelled a cushion with her feet, hating how stupid it sounded even if only in her head.

She'd fallen in love with the boss.

How many times had she warned friends away from the perils of getting involved with workmates? Don't screw the crew. Everyone knew it was an unwritten law, hence her agreeing to Bo's blunt ground rules.

How many times had she seen the devastation first-hand when a work relationship soured? Too many in the brief stints she'd done as a waitress and retail assistant while studying for her art degree and she'd vowed to never go there. Surprise,

surprise, here she was, mired in her own little workplace drama though this one was serious.

This one could cost her the dream she'd been striving for, the dream that meant everything.

She'd struggled for so long, saving every cent, but if the mud-brick cottage she coveted sold at next month's auction, she wasn't sure if she could start again. It had taken her forever to find the perfect house, the type of home she could make her own, the epitome of her dream for a lifetime of security.

And now she might have to throw it all away because she'd made one stupid mistake.

Love sucked. Big time.

Making a lightning-fast decision to drop everything and drive to Stockton to take another look at her dream home— one of the few dreams she had left courtesy of a cold-hearted author—she leapt to her feet and flung the cushion at the couch.

However, her sporting prowess had always been average and the cushion missed, hitting a pile of papers and magazines stacked on a small table behind it, sending them cascading to the floor.

Cursing this all-round crappy day, she kneeled and started re-stacking the pile, wondering why Bo hadn't filed these along with the rest of his super-organised office. Then again, why should she care? She wouldn't be working in here beyond the end of the week anyway.

Her eyes landed on the cover of a financial magazine and she grabbed it, eager to take a closer look. There was a familiarity about Wynn Burrell, the face of finance in Australia, the guy who owned half the country via his massive financial holdings.

The Burrell's were huge, particularly in Sydney, and had been plastered on every magazine and newspaper around the world. Wynn's profile sold newspapers and magazines, not that she could blame the media. He had a striking face, more rugged than classically handsome, with his large nose, chiselled cheekbones and penetrating green eyes. Eyes the same colour as Bo's, featured in a tiny picture boxed to the right. The same tiny box that proclaimed Bo as Wynn's son.

No way...

She flipped to the accompanying article and sped-read, her eyes scanning the print as fast as she could, eager to learn as much about the guy who obviously had more secrets than she had pairs of jeans.

The article centred on Wynn and his mega-success in the finance world but toward the end there was speculation regarding Wynn 'The Whiz's' son Bogart, who was well on the way to following in dear dad's footsteps but vanished from the business scene years ago without a word. Wynn said he was proud of his son and the choices he'd made and he expected the media to respect his privacy.

That was the gist of it and Tahnee flipped the magazine shut, her gaze drawn to Bo's picture.

Why hadn't he told her?

They'd chatted so many times about his past and his dad, yet he hadn't mentioned a word of his true identity.

"What's going on with you?" she muttered, rattling the magazine, wishing she could rattle some sense into Bo in the process.

Staring at his pic, she traced the outline of his confident, smiling face with her finger, wondering if she really knew this guy at all.

In actual fact, what did she know?

Bo didn't like socialising and had turned into a recluse.

Bo didn't like getting emotionally attached.

Bo was brilliant at his job but lousy at relationships.

The weird thing was, now she'd learned Wynn Burrell was

Bo's father, several things clicked into place like toppling dominoes.

He valued his privacy? She could live with that.

He wanted to protect his identity? She could live with that too.

He didn't trust her enough to tell her important stuff like who he really was? No way could she live with that.

But learning the truth about his identity gave her an idea... a tiny flicker of hope ignited in her heart and burned brighter, fanned by optimism. What if she could get Bo to open up to her, to realise she accepted him for who he was? Would that mean a possible future for them?

After yesterday morning, she'd never wanted to see the guy again let alone admit her love for him but now she couldn't ignore the possibility of obtaining her dream after all.

She'd already gone out on a limb.

What did she have to lose?

―――

Bo cursed when he swung into the drive and saw the kitchen light on. Tahnee was up. When he'd come home at the same time last night the house had been in darkness and he'd welcomed the silence as he'd slipped in unnoticed.

He didn't want to see her, especially in the kitchen, the place they'd sat around every night after work, drinking coffee, feigning interest in food before tearing each other's clothes off and barely making it to his room.

He parked the car, switched off the ignition and grabbed his laptop. He couldn't ignore her forever. They had three days left to work together, three days to make this book his best work ever, three days for him to figure out what he'd do if she chose to walk out on him and leave him without an illustrator—and a gaping hole in his life he didn't want to contemplate.

Eager to get the inevitable confrontation over and done with, he let himself into the house and stepped into the kitchen, every muscle in his body screaming to run while he still could because every time he saw Tahnee he slipped further into a place he didn't want to go.

The place that painted this very picture before his eyes: a beautiful, warm, vibrant woman waiting for him in his cosy kitchen at the end of a long hard day. A place that beckoned and could suck him in forever if he let it.

"You're still up," he said, stalking into the kitchen with all the finesse of an angry bear, before dumping his laptop and heading for the fridge.

Not that he wanted anything to drink but if he didn't have something to fill his hands he'd be tempted to grab hold of her and never let go. She'd looked incredible earlier that morning, all fresh and sunny and vibrant, and it had taken all his willpower not to haul her into his arms, which is why he'd headed out to work for the day.

Work, ha. Like that would happen while he had his mind focussed on one thing and one thing only; figuring out how to clean up the mess he'd made of his relationship with Tahnee.

"Hello to you too," she said, her voice a husky purr, and his head snapped up, hitting the top shelf of the fridge.

What had happened to the frosty tone, the one he could deal with? She hadn't sounded like this since...well, since he'd been buried inside her losing his mind.

After grabbing a soda, he swung to face her. "What's with the tone?"

She widened her eyes slightly, doing a great innocent act if he didn't already know better. For a girl who looked like butter wouldn't melt in her mouth, that same mouth was definitely built for sin.

"No tone. I need to chat to you about some interesting publicity stuff I saw on you today."

"Where?" He ripped the tab off the soda and took several gulps, hoping to ease the tightness in his throat muscles which had seized the second he started focussing on her mouth.

"A financial magazine. The one with you and your dad on the cover."

He choked on the fizzy bubbles, coughing and spluttering like a drowning man. Ironic, considering he felt like he was floundering way out of his depth the instant he heard she'd discovered his real identity.

He cleared his throat several times before answering. "Guess we can add snooping to your CV."

Her silky smile didn't assuage his fear there was more to this conversation than her discovery. "If you don't want me to know who you really are, you shouldn't leave stuff lying around." She paused, her gaze steely. "You should tell me."

"It's not important," he said, finishing off the soda and lobbing it into the trash, wishing he could slam dunk this conversation as easily.

"Not to you, obviously."

She wasn't cutting him any slack, pinning him with a direct stare that could freeze ice in Antarctica. Propping against a bench-top, he said, "I've already told you I'm a private person. I barely know you, why would I divulge my true identity to you?"

She flinched as if he'd struck her and he gripped the bench before he wavered, lost resolve, and rushed over to comfort her as was his first impulse.

He knew where this was leading now. She wanted to push him to open up, get him to acknowledge the feelings he had for her simmering away like a bubbling volcano ready to explode. But he wouldn't let that happen. He wouldn't do that to her. She was too special to be lumbered with a guy who couldn't give her half of what she wanted.

To her credit, she didn't bail him up about not knowing her, about belittling the incredible time they'd shared together. Instead, she blinked several times before resuming her killer glare.

"Nice try, but I'm not going to let your signature moodiness stop me. So you're a Burrell? Big deal. I don't understand why it's a secret."

Damn it, he hated feeling like this, hated having to justify his motivations. This is why he didn't do relationships. This is why he'd really left the financier life behind. He liked being on his own, he liked doing things his way.

Though he'd loved working alongside his old man and Brennan, he'd hated having to justify every little thing he did: to his boss, to the board, and to his dad, who had never questioned his judgement before.

Even as a kid, he'd been a loner, preferring to concoct stories in his head rather than play footy and though he was grateful for the years he'd put into finance, the years that had allowed him to set up this house to follow his dream to write in the first place, he didn't miss the whole 'why are you doing that, Bo' routine.

Yet here he was, five years later, having to explain himself and it didn't sit well.

"No big secret. None of this is any of your business, that's why I didn't tell you."

He pushed away from the bench and headed for the door. He didn't want to go through this any longer, didn't want to say something he'd regret.

"Funny, I didn't pick you for a guy who'd run scared."

He stopped dead and turned to face her. "You don't know the first thing about me."

To his surprise, she shot to her feet and crossed the short

distance between them in a second, almost treading on his toes while she got in his face.

"That's bull. I know I see a guy who won't acknowledge any emotion whatsoever. A guy so wrapped up in hiding from the world he can't see what's standing right in front of him—"

"You want to know what I see standing in front of me? I'll tell you. I see a nosy woman who doesn't know when to quit, a woman who pushes and prods and has to know every damn thing even if it has nothing to do with her. A woman who should leave well enough alone."

She paled, her blue eyes stark, but he couldn't let a flash of pity for her stop what he had to do. In a way, this hadn't come at a better time. He hadn't meant to say half of that, the words spilling out in anger, but it was too late. The damage was done and she stared at him like he was some kind of monster.

He could've bundled her into his arms and apologised. He could've told her the truth about what being a Burrell meant: stubborn, proud and ambitious, three traits that didn't bode well for family life, traits that could ultimately kill emotion, and he had them in spades.

He'd been too stubborn to acknowledge his true dream years earlier when he could've saved himself years of grinding away in a dead-end career.

He'd been too proud to accept his father's help when he'd finally made the break.

And his relentless ambition to get to the top of his profession and stay there is what drove him every day, what woke his muse in the morning and what would ultimately drive away any person stupid enough to get close to him.

At the first glimpse of tears in her eyes, he took a step back, ready to end this conversation here and now. "I don't appreciate you interfering in my life so butt out."

Pain warred with pity and the pain won out, her stare shimmering with tears and acting like a sucker punch to his gut. She felt sorry for him for being such a heartless bastard. And he'd hurt her more than he wanted to.

"I guess that's been the problem all along. You don't appreciate me much, period."

She pushed past him and ran for the flat, her sandals clattering against the floorboards in loud, staccato sounds like a hammer driving inch-long nails into his heart.

Thirteen

Wally liked being organised. A place for everything and everything in its place. However, today his burrow seemed too tidy, too stark. He liked it when Prue the platypus or Eddy the echidna dropped by for a cup of billy tea or a bit of bush tucker. However, today he particularly wanted to see one visitor but Kaz had vanished. She'd been so mad at him last night. He'd thought about digging all the way to Tasmania but he couldn't even summon the energy to do that.

Bo Bradford's blog.

Seeing the note propped against his computer didn't surprise Bo in the least as he entered the office, rubbing a hand over his gritty eyes. He hadn't slept all night, his head filled with images of the lousy way he'd treated Tahnee.

She hadn't deserved his wrath, and no matter how much he wanted to avoid the personal twist their relationship had taken, he shouldn't have driven her away like that.

They were a good team, dynamic business partners, and he'd probably ruined what little chance he had of patching their working relationship because of a childish bout of temper.

He snatched the note and unfolded it, her bold, flowing script indicative of the vitality of the woman who'd penned it.

BO,

I'LL BE WORKING FROM MY SISTER'S APARTMENT UNTIL THE END OF THE WEEK AND THE CONCLUSION OF OUR BUSINESS ARRANGEMENT. YOU CAN EMAIL ME THE LAST TWO WALLY SCENES AT THE EMAIL ADDRESS ON MY CV. I'LL FINISH THE REMAINING SKETCHES AND GET THEM BACK TO YOU. WAGES DUE CAN BE DEPOSITED INTO MY BANK ACCOUNT.

BEST OF LUCK WITH YOUR WRITING,

TAHNEE.

He crumpled the note in his fist, hating the finality of her words, hating the way his heart lurched more.

He'd botched it.

Well and truly screwed up the greatest opportunity to land in his lap ever. For a guy who had a way with words, he sure hadn't found the right ones to use with Tahnee.

That's when it hit him. Fair and square, right between the eyes, a knock-out punch and he staggered back and collapsed into his chair like a prize-fighter on the ropes for the last time.

Her note was all business; plain-speaking and to the point as Tahnee had always been with him, yet when he'd thought about the greatest opportunity a second ago, business had been furthest from his mind. He'd been thinking about losing her, every delicious, sassy, outspoken inch of her, and it left him struggling for air.

But if the soul-deep emptiness spreading through him wasn't about business, that meant...

He groaned, shaking his head, hoping the rapid movement

might clear it. It didn't and he had a sneaking suspicion nothing would until he admitted the truth.

He loved her.

The stupidest, dumbest move a guy like him could make, a guy who valued his independence above all else, a guy who didn't have the foggiest idea how to be part of a couple, a guy too wrapped up in his fantasy world creating fictional characters to take a risk and enter the real world again.

He couldn't love her.

He'd never experienced the much-touted emotion with a woman let alone knew what it was. How could a guy who'd never known love identify it?

Closing his eyes, he dredged up every memory he could that he equated with his version of love: his first Christmas, age four, when his dad had taken a whole day off work to spend with the family. The first time he'd ridden a horse, the first time his folks had come to watch him play footy, his first kiss at age ten with an older twelve year old, and the many times he'd seen genuine affection in his dad's eyes around the offices at Burrell Finance.

His only experience with love had been the familial kind, where parents and siblings accepted him for who he was regardless if he was a major pain in the ass or not. As for women...he knew jack.

Not surprising, Kay didn't feature in his warm and fuzzy memories. She'd been an accessory to his life back then, the type of girlfriend who wanted to get ahead rather than get serious. Love hadn't entered the equation and he hadn't missed it at the time.

Unlike now, when the thought of never seeing Tahnee again, of not hearing her contagious laugh, of not seeing her sleepy, half-smile first thing in the morning, of never holding her or tasting her or making love to her ever again, acted like a kick in the guts, leaving him sick and sorry.

He'd already paid the ultimate price in seeing a lot less of his family while following his dream. What if shutting himself off from the world cost him the woman he loved too?

He had to do something before it was too late.

———

Tahnee opened the door to Kristen's apartment, stepped into it and sagged with relief.

She'd done it.

Walking away from Bo should've been the hardest thing in the world but he'd made it easy for her last night. She should be thanking him.

Instead, she dropped her bags at the door, slammed it shut and headed for the sofa, curling onto her side while battling tears. Wriggling, she tried to get comfortable but her sister's trendy chrome-legged, leather combo was built for looks, not comfort. Unlike Bo's, where she'd happily curled up every day, working with bursts of creativity she'd never experienced before.

"Stop it," she muttered, grabbing a cushion and hugging it tight. She'd told herself on the way over here she wouldn't do this. She wouldn't think about him, wouldn't dwell on the last ten days or dredge up the endless store of memories of the time they'd spent together.

She had a job to do. She was a professional and she always delivered her work on time. She had a reputation as a businesswoman and one of the best at that. No way would she let a teensy-weensy broken heart stand in her way.

She burst into tears.

With angry swipes at the useless tears trickling down her cheeks she got up, flung the cushion away and grabbed her bag. She needed a distraction and right now, answering the gazillion text messages Carissa had left her seemed a good idea.

Her sister would be frantic by now but Tahnee had been so caught up in the drama of the last few days she hadn't been able to text Carissa let alone respond to her three voice messages. Besides, the last time they'd spoken had been over coffee, when she'd envisaged a rosy future and Carissa had been one hundred percent supportive as usual.

Tahnee knew if she didn't respond soon, Carissa would more than likely arrive on Bo's doorstep. Not a good idea, considering Tahnee had moved out and now taken up residence in her jet-setting sister Kristen's apartment. Ironic, considering Carissa had holed up here when her now-husband Brody hadn't realised they had a future.

Not that she was expecting similar miracles from Bo. He had as much chance of showing up on her doorstep with a marriage proposal as she did of climbing the Harbour Bridge; an impossibility considering her fear of heights.

She picked up her phone and contemplated calling Carissa for all of two seconds before realising it was a dumb idea. Her sister would hear her choked voice and blocked nose, Tahnee would start bawling again, and having her overzealous sister drive down here to ply her with tissues and advice was not what she needed right now. She needed time to recover, time to finish her work, and time to get herself together before she went home.

Aware she had to tell Carissa something to assuage her sister's concern, she composed a message at odds with her churned up, blubbering self.

Hey C,
Sorry I've been silent. Busy with work. Can't talk now.
Tell all when I see you.
T xx

Hitting the send button, she waited for the almost instant response she expected from her curious sister. The phone beeped a second later and she managed a rueful smile. Carissa must've had the phone glued to her hand to have answered that quickly.

You're bad. I was worried.
Sure you're okay?
When will I see you?
C xox

Sooner than Carissa thought considering Tahnee's dream job had withered and died along with her hopes for a future with the dream man.

Though maybe she'd stay here a while longer, a week or two after she'd handed in the final sketches. No use rushing back to Stockton where Carissa would smother her in personal remedies for the broken-hearted: copious amounts of chocolate, Kahlua, and romance novels to try and prove love really did conquer all.

She'd laughed when Carissa had forced her pick-me-up packs on the lovelorn of Stockton before but now she would be the intended recipient it wasn't so funny anymore. And exactly why she'd headed for the anonymity of Kristen's apartment rather than heading home.

Anonymity...great, maybe she'd caught the emotionless hermit disease from Bo?

She had to reassure Carissa once and for all, then she could get down to the serious business of wallowing in peace.

I'm OK, see you soon.
I'll call.
T xx

Thankfully, Carissa got the message and Tahnee's cell remained silent so she tossed it in her bag, lay back on the sofa and closed her eyes, determined not to waste one more tear on a guy who didn't deserve them.

Now, if she could erase her memories of the last week and a half when she'd had the time of her life, she'd be happy.

Bo had wasted an hour trying to come up with a suitable response to Tahnee's note, something that wouldn't sound too strong, too weak, or too desperate. A hard task considering he had to see her and explain, but the words wouldn't flow and for the umpteenth time over the last few days he stared at a blank screen.

He hated having to email her such an important message when he'd much rather talk face to face. Calling wasn't an option as he'd end up saying the wrong thing again. Besides, she probably wouldn't answer and he didn't blame her.

He remembered her mentioning she had a sister working overseas who kept an apartment in Sydney but for the life of him he couldn't remember where. Not that it would do him much good. She'd probably slam the door in his face if he had the audacity to show up unannounced after the way he'd last spoken to her.

Damn, he'd treated her badly. He'd been selfish as usual, putting his needs first, ramming home his point of view to assert the upper hand. But he wasn't in the financial world any more and he didn't have to prove anything to anybody, particularly not to a woman who had laid her heart on the line for him and he'd trampled it without a second thought.

He'd spent too long holed up in this place trying to forge a career and follow his dream, allowing it to take precedence over everything, including having a life. He needed to wake up and smell the bush flowers like his good mate Wally.

He needed to get a life.

Propelled into action, he typed a quick, honest email to Tahnee before he had time to mull over it.

Hey Tahnee,
Sorry for the way things ended.
I mucked up. Big time. Would like a chance to explain?

How about joining Kaz, Prue, Eddy and Wally at my place for a chat? Or the gang can come to you, whichever's easiest?

Hope to hear from you soon.

Bo

It wasn't his best work but he hoped the humour would give him a shot at breaking through her defences, which she had every right to erect after the way he'd treated her. Pushing her away had been a reaction born of years of hibernation. Time to change the rules, shake things up and see what happened.

He hit the send key and waited at the computer for the next ten minutes, desperate to hear an answering beep that he had a response. Instead, deafening silence, and he idly scanned his latest online bookstore rankings with little interest. Who cared about sales when he'd potentially ruined the best thing to ever happen to him?

What seemed like an eternity later, his computer beeped, signalling he had email, and his hand shook as he opened his inbox to see if Tahnee had responded. Holding his breath, he punched the air when he saw an email from her.

You bet you mucked up.

You made a right Wally of yourself!

I'm willing to see you grovel on Friday once these final scenes are complete.

I'll drop them off at your place at six.

But don't expect miracles.

Tahnee

He reread her email five times, trying to decipher it. Was she still mad as hell or thawing?

She'd attempted humour with the Wally comment but what did she mean by miracles? Was she referring to her work on the final part of the book or forgiving him for acting like a jerk?

This was exactly why he didn't do emotions. They confused him the hell out of him.

After sending a brief "great, see you then," response, he swung out of his chair and headed for the door. He needed to clear his clogged head and a swim should do the trick. Hopefully it would also help him figure out how on earth to convince the woman he loved to take a chance on a guy like him.

Fourteen

Wally spent all day fixing the new hole he'd dug. Kaz was coming for a visit. He hadn't seen her in ages and he'd missed her. If he was really, really nice to her, maybe she'd want to stick around? He'd like that. His new digs were no fun without her. What would convince her to stay? He'd thought long and hard before coming up with a brilliant idea. Kaz loved chocolate topping. Maybe if he bought her a crate of the stuff...

Bo Bradford's blog.

As Tahnee buzzed the intercom at Bo's front gate, she closed her eyes and leant back against the headrest.

She had to be nuts.

Crazy, mad, certifiable, to be doing this.

What was she thinking?

As the gates swung open, she knew the answer. She wasn't thinking. Ever since she'd entered these gates two weeks ago her brain had gone into hibernation and no amount of coaxing could bring her common sense out.

She should've deleted Bo's email the moment it hit her inbox.

She should've ignored it or practised rude replies without sending them before deleting.

She should've told him to stick it.

Instead, here she was, dolled up in her favourite white denim hipsters, tight pink T-shirt, and enough mascara and lip gloss to give her a confidence boost, ready to march into enemy territory, pretend she didn't give a damn and steel herself against whatever pitiful excuses he might give for his behaviour, before heading back to Stockton. Definitely crazy.

She pulled up at the front door, parked, and ignored the strong wave of déjà vu. She grabbed her bag with the final sketches and headed for the house, rung the bell and waited, hating the feeling of being a visitor when she'd learned to treat this place like her own.

Strange, considering she never took to houses quickly. She had her dream home in mind and nowhere else lived up to it yet, Bo's house had drawn her in, made her feel welcome and secure, a surprise in itself. She never felt secure, no matter how successful her career or how much money she earned or how many friends she had. It never seemed enough, yet she'd felt secure here, in this house, in this guy's arms.

The guy who opened the door and smiled at her like she were the best present he'd ever received.

"I brought your sketches."

It sucked as an opening line but all she could manage on the spur of the moment. Besides, witty repartee wasn't her forte when her mind zeroed straight to the gutter, remembering how good Bo looked, particularly without the jeans and polo he wore.

"Great, come on in."

She brushed past him, head held high, senses reeling as she

caught the familiar smell of his aftershave, the subtle blend of spice and oak imprinted on her receptors forever.

Clamping down on the overwhelming desire to drop the sketches at the door and either run or jump him, she marched toward the kitchen before belatedly realising it probably wasn't the best place to meet. Too much had happened in that kitchen: too many memories, too many opportunities to slip up and act on them...

Taking a steadying breath, she stepped into the kitchen, headed for the table and whipped out her sketches. The sooner they focussed on business and she got out of here, clothes and dignity intact, the better.

"Can I get you anything?" He propped against a bench, wearing the same, sexy smile that had robbed her of every ounce of common sense she'd ever had and she bit back her instant response of 'you.'

She shook her head, pointing to the sketches. "Your final two scenes were brilliant. Hope I've done them justice."

He crossed the kitchen and stood next to her, invading her personal space, sending her crazy. She was supposed to be mad at this guy. She was supposed to hate him for not loving her, for being so business-oriented, for seeing their only connection beyond today as a work 'arrangement'.

But the longer he stood there, radiating a potent heat enticing her to lean toward him, she couldn't think of anything bar how much she wanted to sweep her work onto the floor and have her way with him on the table.

"These are great. You've excelled yourself."

Easy for him to say. She'd been up all night putting the finishing touches to the sketches, determined to show him how professional she could be when all she wanted to do was smash the sketches over his head.

"Good. Now that's finished I'll be leaving—"

"What did you think of the ending?"

She finally looked up and met his gaze for the first time, hating the treacherous lurch of her heart as dazzling green connected with confused blue.

"The ending was cute, like all your books."

His gaze never wavered, boring into her as if trying to convey some hidden message she couldn't comprehend. "Yeah, but did you like how Wally and Kaz finally got their act together?"

A light-bulb went off in her head. He couldn't be serious. Surely he wasn't implying he was Wally and she was Kaz? But that would mean he wanted a happy ending for them...as if.

"The ending was good but personally I thought Wally was too much of a dufus for a smart kangaroo like Kaz. She should've kicked him to the watering hole for acting how he did for so long."

His face fell and she almost laughed out loud. This was too easy.

"Don't you think Wally deserved points for coming to his senses before it was too late?"

She shook her head. "Nah...Kaz let him off too easy. He was an emotionally-repressed, uptight waddler and she had more spunk in her tail than he did in his whole neurotic body. She should never have given him a second chance. He didn't deserve it."

Bo stared at her, horror mingling with regret in his eyes and she couldn't contain the laughter bubbling up any longer.

He frowned as she doubled over. "What's so funny?"

"You are," she gasped, holding her sides and laughing harder. "*Wally*."

His frown lingered for a second longer before fading away, the corners of his mouth twitching until he laughed too. "I'm that transparent?"

"You're a pane of glass," she said, her chuckles petering out as she straightened, wishing they could stay like this forever. Close, happy, sharing a funny moment in a cosy room that held great memories.

But this wasn't a fantasy and memories had a way of fading when not sustained, a bit like their relationship, over before it had begun thanks to him.

"So there's no chance of a happy ending for us?"

She stared him down, hating the flicker of hope in her heart. "Sorry, but as I've already told you, I can't accept your offer to work with you."

His eyes widened in surprise. "I'm not talking about work."

Then what the heck was he talking about? He couldn't be talking about...her pulse accelerated to breakneck speed.

"I'm talking about us and the possibility you want to throw every rule out the window and start over."

Shock made her jaw drop but before she could respond, he continued.

"Before you say anything, I need to apologise for the way I reacted after you found out my true identity. You were only being curious and I acted like a jerk. I'm sorry."

"Apology accepted."

Now, could they get back to the good stuff? The part where he wanted to start over?

"I owe you an explanation."

"You owe me nothing." She couldn't give a flying fig about his identity when there were larger matters at stake, namely her heart. "Apart from two weeks wages, that is."

A rueful smile crossed his face. "After putting up with my boorish behaviour, you deserve a year's worth. But I do want to explain some stuff to you."

He'd said the right thing and sucked her in. She couldn't

walk away from unravelling a good mystery any more than she could walk away from him.

"Go ahead," she said, hoping she hadn't given him license to explain away his behaviour and kill her hopes for their future once and for all.

"Being a Burrell is great. People have always bowed and scraped and opened doors because of who I am and the family I was lucky enough to be born into. When I wanted to write, I needed to prove something to myself, that I could succeed in something without having anyone give me a helping hand along the way because I was Bo Burrell. So I swore my dad and Brennan to secrecy, bought this place with the money I'd made through financing and dropped out of society. I didn't want any favours, even from my dad, and I wanted to make it on my own. I love writing but I reckon I chose this profession for a reason, for the solitude and lack of people contact, which I'd had enough of anyway. It felt so damn good to walk away from it all and thankfully my family understood. Now I hope you can."

He snagged her hand and she didn't have the heart to tug it away. Not that she minded the sizzle of electricity from his touch or the warmth it evoked but she couldn't give in too easily. What if this was a ploy to suck her back in to work for him? Surely he wouldn't stoop that low?

"Being an author is everything I dreamed of but I've paid a price. I can't spend time with my family in public anymore because people will hound them for the truth behind my 'disappearance'. I can't go sailing with my dad and Brennan like I used to, I can't hang out or drop by the office for a chat. It's been tough but I've handled it by shutting myself away and focussing on the good side of being a recluse. That's why I don't post pics online. And only a select few in the publishing industry know my real identity and they keep it hush-hush."

"So you're never recognised at parties like the one we went to?"

He shook his head. "My hair's longer now and a different colour. Besides, people only see what they want to see. To the publishing world, I'm a reclusive author. How could I ever be one of the money-making Burrell's?"

He paused. "I liked being a hermit. Then you came along, and you encapsulate everything I'm afraid of. You're vivacious and bubbly and you love people. You thrive in the company of others and I saw it first-hand at the awards night. You shine and dazzle whereas I've been there done that, never want to return. And worse, you bring out that side of me. You make me want to have fun and play and live for the moment, a scary proposition for a shy guy like me. But it's time I stopped hiding away, time to join the real world, with you by my side hopefully."

He squeezed her hand, his eyes imploring her to understand, to forgive, and the ice around her heart thawed a tad.

"Pretty big turnaround. What brought it on?"

She should be doing cartwheels he'd opened up and even better, wanted her in his life other than as a colleague. But she couldn't shake the feeling there was more, some piece of this puzzle that didn't fit.

He shrugged, his expression sheepish. "We're a great team, not just in the office. Guess it took me a while to figure it out."

And just like that, the final, odd-shaped piece slid into place, completing the picture and leaving her more devastated than before.

He was referring to the amazing sex they'd had. He missed it and wanted them to get back into the swing of things. How could she have been so stupid? Again.

He hadn't mentioned a relationship or love or any of the words she'd wanted to hear. Uh-uh. He wasn't getting any and he wanted her back. What did he think, she'd pop in for a quickie whenever she was in Sydney?

Fury surged through her body and she yanked her hand out of his, fumbling for her bag and knocking it to the floor in her haste. Cursing, she bent to retrieve the contents now scattered across the floor and he helped her, handing her a pen, chewing gum and a tampon while she blushed and snatched it out of his hand.

"Hey, I know this is a surprise but I thought you might want to talk about it, see where we go from here, maybe give it another go?"

"I bet you did," she muttered, standing and slinging her bag over her shoulder, wishing she'd worn flats rather than heels so she could make a run for the door. "Sorry, I'm not in the mood anymore."

Confusion clouded his eyes and she snorted in disgust. "Cut the act. Or do you want me to spell it out for you?"

Hugging her bag to her chest like a shield, she said, "Fine, I'll spell it out for you. I'm not interested. Got it?"

He stepped back as if she'd physically struck him, pain slashing his face.

"Loud and clear," he said, staring at her like she'd morphed into a two-headed monster. "I won't bother you again."

"Good."

She willed her feet to move but for some reason they didn't respond as she stared at him like an onlooker at a car accident, hating the devastation but unable to look away.

For a guy who'd received a knock-back, he looked pretty cut up about it. Worse, he looked like someone had died. Good, now he knew what she felt like inside as her heart shrivelled for the last time.

"It's only sex. Don't worry, a guy like you will have no trouble finding a replacement for me."

His head snapped up as he took a step toward her. "What did you say?"

Rolling her eyes, she wondered if he was doing this whole obtuse act on purpose as a way to gain sympathy. "You heard me. I guess a city boy like you thought a country girl like me might enjoy a booty call every time she came into town but trust me, you'd be better off finding someone nearer to home, someone to call on whenever you get the urge."

Shaking his head, he grabbed her arms. "I can't believe you just said that." The pain in his eyes struck anew. "I can't believe you think I'm like that."

A niggle of doubt wormed its way into her head. Was she wrong? Had she jumped to conclusions to explain away her own feelings of inadequacy?

"What am I supposed to think? You talk about picking up where we left off, how we're a good team out of the office as well as in it. The way I see it, the only other teamwork we did out of office hours involved sex, so I made a logical assumption."

Pain leeched from his steady stare only to be replaced by sadness. "You could think I'm the kind of guy who wouldn't treat you like that. You could think I'm interested in more than your body. You could think I'm hinting at a relationship but hey, maybe I've been holed up in this house so long I'm talking in riddles and expecting you to understand."

Her heart tripped and flipped. "Did you just say relationship?"

Maybe guys used relationship these days as a euphemism for affair or fling or whatever it was they called no-strings-attached sex?

He released her arms to capture her face between his hands, heat blazing from his eyes and warming her better than the Bondi sun on a hot summer's day.

"I can see I'm going to have to spell this out for you."

Brushing her cheeks with his thumbs, trailing his fingertips along her jaw, he said, "I love you. I want a relationship with you. Hell, I want to marry you and watch you stub your toes and give yourself concussion and do all the other nutty things you do because I'm crazy about you. There, is that clear enough for you?"

Pure, indescribable joy filled her and she lunged at him, plastering her lips to his, kissing him until she couldn't breathe.

When they came up for airs, he said, "I take it you like the idea?"

She laughed and hugged him tighter. "For an author, you have a lousy way with words. Why didn't you say all that stuff at the start?"

His sexy grin set her pulse racing again. "And make it easy for you? Where's the fun in that?"

She swatted him, wrapping her arms around his waist, secure in his embrace, knowing there was no place else she'd rather be. "You do know I love you too, right?"

"Right."

"And I want to make babies with you?"

His grin turned goofy. "Uh…okay."

"And I've got my heart set on the whole white picket fence, mud-brick cottage dream in my home town?"

"How about we spend some time there, some time here?"

She pretended to think for a moment, capitulating when he tickled her ribs. "Fine. And you know there'll be a new set of ground rules?"

He nuzzled her neck, kissing his way to her mouth where she welcomed his hot, open-mouth kiss, heat turning her body to liquid fire.

"No more rules," he murmured against the side of her mouth, trailing his lips along her cheek to her earlobe where he nibbled and nipped until she squealed.

Placing her hands on his chest, she bunched his T-shirt in her fingers. "Hey, don't you know the best part about rules?"

"What?"

"They're meant to be broken."

She laughed as he hauled her into his arms and proceeded to show her exactly how.

Epilogue

Wally liked having two homes. He liked the trips between burrows, he liked having friends at both watering holes but best of all he liked having Kaz around. She made him laugh, she made him the best bush tucker dinners, but most of all she made him feel like the luckiest wombat in the whole of Australia. Kaz was the coolest.

Bo Bradford's blog, three months later.

"How's that final sketch coming along?"

Tahnee glanced up from her sketchpad to find Bo smiling at her from behind his laptop. "You're a slave-driver."

He held up his hands in protest. "Hey, I wasn't the one who impressed the bosses so much at the awards night they offered us a three book contract with killer deadlines."

"Yeah, but you could've warned me I'd be constantly distracted and find it difficult to work." Her gaze roved over him, from his upper body clearly delineated in pale blue cotton to his bare legs poking out from camel-coloured shorts under the desk, her pulse humming in anticipation of another 'distraction'.

His grin widened as he clasped hands and stretched overhead. "You find me distracting, huh?"

"I find you irresistible." She threw her sketchpad down and crossed to the desk to straddle his lap and wrap her arms around his neck. "And if we keep doing this, we're never going to make deadline."

His hands skimmed her back as his head dipped for a quick kiss so he could murmur against the side of her mouth, "I do my best work under pressure. How about you?"

"I can't think when you're doing that," she said, making a soft mewl of pleasure as he slipped his hands under her top and his fingertips danced across her skin.

"That's the whole point."

He kissed her, the type of drugging, seductive fusion of lips that left her breathless and hot and turned on, craving his touch like she'd never get enough.

Sighing with regret, she broke the kiss. "You know I have to finish that last sketch right now, don't you?"

He nodded, an impish gleam in his eyes. "Yeah, I know. Just think how much fun we're going to have celebrating later. I have a crateful of chocolate topping waiting for us."

"You're a bad man."

"And you love me for it. Particularly my creative side which comes up with new, inventive ways to use it."

Knowing she'd go into complete meltdown any second now, she brushed her lips across his. "Hold that thought."

She reluctantly disengaged from his arms and padded back to the sofa, his soft chuckles following her. Easy for him to laugh. He hadn't turned into a raving nymphomaniac, the type of woman who wanted sex all the time, even when the man of her dreams so much as glanced her way.

She sat on the sofa, picked up her sketchpad and held it

up, determined not to look at him. No easy feat considering she couldn't keep her hands or her eyes off him these days. The last few months had been a dream come true: working together, playing together, more playing together…

She hadn't bought the mud-brick cottage, with negotiations taking longer than expected, but it didn't bother her. Being with Bo, surrounded by his love on a daily basis, she'd finally realised security wasn't about bricks and mortar or having a nest-egg the size of an island. The unconditional, unswerving love of one guy had done more for her insecurities than any house ever could.

"Sorry to interrupt but there's an email here from Carissa, sent high priority, her third one of the day? What do you want me to do?"

She peeped over her pad for a second, like staring at an eclipse. Any longer and she'd get burned for sure. At least, her body would burn up and she'd be forced to take off her clothes and they'd be right back to where they'd started: possibly missing a deadline for the first time because they couldn't keep their hands off each other.

"You know she thinks our lives run parallel to Wally and Kaz?"

"Yeah."

"And she's glued to your blog for daily updates?"

"Yeah."

"Well, she's been giving me a hard time lately about wedding stuff. Why don't we give our matron of honour a little something to stew over?"

Bo's eyes lit up. He had a great rapport with Carissa and loved dishing it out as much as he took it from her, and it looked like he was up for a bit of teasing as Tahnee hoped.

"Great idea. Leave it with me."

Sending him a wink, she concentrated on putting the final touches on Wally and Kaz's outback party, complete with bush band and gum tree marquee. After ten minutes hard slog where she refused to think of her sexy fiancé let alone look at him, she finally threw down her charcoal, leapt to her feet and practically ran across the room.

"I'm finished."

He smiled and opened his arms to her. "Funny, I'm just getting started."

His sizzling glance scorched her from the inside out and she took the best seat in the house; his lap.

"Me too, but I want to see what you sent Carissa first."

Chuckling, he swung her around to face the laptop, his arms circled snugly around her waist.

"Take a look."

With a click of the mouse, Bo's blog came up, with Wally, Kaz, Prue and co. doing happy dances around the borders of the screen.

Tahnee scanned the page for the latest update, her eyes widening with delight when she spotted it.

WALLY WOULD LIKE WENDY THE WALLABY TO STOP NOSING AROUND HIS BURROW. KAZ IS GETTING JUMPY, WHAT WITH A POSSIBLE JOEY JOINING THE GANG. WALLY KNOWS WENDY IS KAZ'S SISTER BUT MAYBE SHE SHOULD HOP TO IT FOR NOW AND NOSE AROUND SOMEWHERE ELSE?

She laughed and swung to face him. "You didn't really post that on your blog, did you? You can't lie like that."

He shook his head, joining in her laughter. "No. That's just the template I sent to Carissa."

"You've done it now."

His eyes darkened as he traced a finger ever-so-slowly down her cheek. "Not yet. But I'm about to..."

Desire pooled deep within as she brushed a kiss across his lips. "I have a few rules. Rule number one: must say 'I love you' to future wife before having amazing sex with her."

"I love you," he murmured, tracing her lips in the barest of kisses. "What's rule number two?"

"Must draw out foreplay as long as possible to drive future wife mad with lust for her sexy future husband."

"How's this for a start?"

A familiar shiver of awareness rippled through her body as his hands traced lazy circles in the middle of her back, moving with slow, exquisite precision downward, lower and lower until he touched her butt and settled her firmly over his bulging erection.

"How's this for obeying the rules?"

She melted under the onslaught of his hot, urgent kiss, his tongue delving into her mouth, challenging her to join in the agonisingly sweet build-up to the ultimate pleasure he created every time he got her naked and panting with need.

"Wow," she murmured when his lips left hers, searing a path across her cheek to the sensitive hollow below her ear.

"What's rule number three?" He whispered a second before nipping her in a gentle bite that had her arching in desperate need to have more of that special treatment all over her body.

"Rules-schmules," she said, snuggling deeper into his arms, welcoming his caresses, secure in the knowledge she'd finally come home.

If you enjoyed this romance, please consider leaving a review to help new readers discover Nicola's books.

Read Kristen's story, THE GOOD GUY.

Kristen Lewis leads a glamorous life in Singapore as an

executive producer of an exciting travel show. She's driven, focussed and never gives in to impulse; like a one night stand with a sexy stranger.
After being head-hunted by an Australian TV studio, she's shocked to discover her new boss is the guy who rocked her world for that one memorable night.

Nathan Boyd is a go-getter entrepreneur. Focussing on work is the only way he knows how to cope with his grief. When he discovers Kris, the first woman to capture his attention in a long time, is now working alongside him, he's thrown.

When Kristen reveals her secret to Nathan, she becomes embroiled in a drama that belongs onscreen rather than off. Will Nate be able to face his fear and take a chance on them?

THE GOOD GUY
EXTRACT

Kristen Lewis had a thing for hotels.

She loved the luxury, the hustle and bustle, even those tiny toiletries designed to slather and splurge and make a weary soul feel like a million dollars for that split second in time.

But most of all she loved the anonymity, where people from all walks of life passed each other without knowing or caring why a successful, thirty-five year old woman at the top of her game would be sitting alone at a bar sipping a spritzer.

"Men," she muttered, stabbing at the lemon wedge in her glass with a swizzle stick, wondering if the ability to blow off other people was a genetic thing. Even as friends they couldn't be trusted.

She took another stab at the piece of lemon, which was starting to resemble Swiss cheese with the number of jabs she'd taken at it in the last five minutes, as she glanced around the bar of the Jazz Hotel in Singapore.

She loved this place, with its sleek chrome lines, trendy black furniture and the occasional splash of red, and had spent many hours here with clients and work colleagues during her four year stint working at a Singaporean TV station. The hotel's grandeur screamed 'special occasion', the reason why she'd chosen to meet Nigel here tonight, envisioning a fun evening with her best work buddy when she'd share her amazing news. Unfortunately, Nigel had a better offer from a twenty-two year old temp and had given her the brush off in the foyer without even hearing her news.

"Buddy my butt," she muttered, taking a sip of her favourite white wine and soda combo as her gaze locked with a guy sitting at the other end of the bar.

Not bad. Dark eyes, dark hair, slight bump in the nose adding character to his handsome face, and sardonic expression highlighted by a slight quirk of his lips at the corners. Almost in a silent challenge, one she had no intention of accepting.

She lowered her gaze quickly and returned to studying coasters while mentally listing Nigel's faults, the main one being he'd ditched her for a temp rather than celebrating the news she'd be returning to Australia shortly. Not that she should be surprised. If Nigel had a choice between wining and dining his latest prospective conquest or sharing a drink with a friend, she lost every time.

Her gaze swept the bar again in and unerringly zeroed in on the good-looking guy. From past experience guys who looked like that sitting alone at a bar made eye contact before moving in for the kill and that's the last thing she needed in her current mood.

Instead, Mr. Handsome stared morosely into his drink, a sombre expression on his striking face and crazily, she sighed in disappointment. She'd never believed in fate or karma or any of that airy-fairy rubbish, yet when she'd locked gazes with the guy a few moments ago something intangible had zinged between them.

Now he wore the same brooding, gloomy expression that matched her mood perfectly and for an irrational second she wondered if she should go over there and share sob stories with him.

With a shake of her head, she finished her spritzer—had to be more wine than soda in it for her to be contemplating such an uncharacteristic action—and scrummaged in her handbag for money.

"Is this yours?"

Looking up from the giant cavernous hole that sucked up purses, tissues, pens, makeup and everything else she needed on a daily basis, making them vanish with a flick of its clasp, she stared into the darkest eyes she'd ever seen, a dark chocolate bordering on black. The stranger she'd made eye contact with earlier now stared at her with polite interest.

"Is this your coat?" His voice, as deep and mysterious as his eyes, washed over her and she blinked, realising he waited for an answer.

"Yes, thanks." She stood, unable to look away, lost in his hypnotic stare.

He had to be pulling some slick, practised move on her and she didn't tolerate guys like that. So why was she standing like a mannequin, stiff and wide-eyed, unable to shake the feeling this guy was on her wavelength.

Smiling, he pointed to the floor. "You knocked it off the back of your stool while searching in that suitcase of yours."

"Suitcase?"

If his eyes mesmerised, they had nothing on his smile, which had her surreptitiously leaning against the bar for support. He pointed to her handbag. "Looks big enough to store the odd suit and a pair of shoes or two."

She laughed and snapped the 'suitcase' shut. "I'm on the go a lot so like to have everything at my fingertips. Important stuff like pens and notebooks and all the other paraphernalia I couldn't possibly find anywhere if I left all this at home."

His smile widened at her sarcasm but somehow it didn't

reach his eyes, a flicker of sadness darkening their depths to almost black and she felt another twinge, an uncharacteristic urge to reach out and comfort him. "Speaking of being on the go, I should catch some sleep. I've got an early plane to catch tomorrow."

"Are you here on business?"

"Yes."

"I live here," she blurted, filled with a desperate urge to keep him talking, to find out more about the mysterious guy who saved her coat from death-by-trampling yet wore an invisible cloak of sadness around his broad shoulders.

"Really? By your Aussie accent I assumed you're here on business too?"

"I could be on holiday," she said, hating the stilted stand up conversation they were having, exactly why she didn't hang out at places like this.

"You're not on holiday."

She raised an eyebrow, surprised by his matter of fact tone. "How do you know that?"

"Because holiday makers have a relaxed look about them, an excited glow, and you don't have it."

"Gee, thanks. So I've lost my glow too," she muttered, wondering what she was doing making small talk with a guy she didn't know and who'd only stopped because she was a klutz.

"You've got a glow," he said, in a tight, strangled tone that made her look up and register the fleeting interest in his eyes. "Just not a holiday one."

Kristen didn't know if it was her bruised ego courtesy of being stood up by Nigel, the spritzer she'd had on an empty stomach, or the nebulous connection she felt for this sad stranger, but she found herself doing something completely out of character.

"If you're not too tired and can hold off on sleep a while longer, maybe you'd like to hear about my non-holiday glow?"

He didn't move, surprise mingling with something else—regret, hope, desire?—in his eyes and she wished the ground would open up as heat surged into her cheeks.

"Forget it. I'm sure you have more important things—"

"I'd like that," he said, hanging her coat over the back of the stool before sliding it out for her.

"Great." She sat, baffled by the simple pleasure derived from his acceptance.

"Would you like a drink?"

"A lemon, lime and bitters, please."

If the splash of wine in the spritzer was responsible for her erratic behaviour, she'd better stick to the soda, otherwise no telling what she might do.

After placing their order with the waiter—who had a knowing smile like he'd seen this scenario a thousand times before—the guy turned to her.

"I'm Nate."

She held out her hand. "Kris. Non-holiday maker. Living in Singapore and loving it."

Warmth enveloped her hand as he shook it with a solid grip. She liked that, hating when guys gave her a limp handshake because of her sex, though she usually showed them, turning their condescension into awe when she wowed them in the business arena.

"Are you living here with family?"

She shook her head, wondering if he was fishing for info about a significant other before ditching the idea. Nate seemed too up-front to play those sorts of games. If he were interested in her romantically he would've asked and sadly, she had a feeling he was sitting here chatting to her out of pity rather than desire for her as a woman. Something in the way he looked at her when she'd invited him to share a drink had clued her in, as if he'd like to refuse but didn't want to hurt her feelings.

She didn't care. Right now, it felt good to talk to someone —she'd been bursting with her news earlier—especially with a guy who looked like Nate, regardless of his motivations for hanging out with a sad case like her.

"No, I don't have much family. Two sisters back in Sydney, that's it. I've been here working, producing one of Singapore's travel shows."

"Sounds interesting."

He thanked the waiter as their drinks were placed in front of them and signed the bill slip, giving her ample opportunity to study him.

White business shirt unbuttoned at the collar and rolled up at the sleeves revealing strong forearms, shirt tucked into the waistband of black trousers encasing long legs ending in a pair of designer shoes. However, the clothes weren't the interesting part, it was the body beneath: lean, streamlined, hinting at subtle strength.

Usually, she wouldn't have given this stranger the time of day let alone invited him to share a drink, yet there was something haunting about Nate, an underlying vulnerability that had her wanting to cuddle him close and pat him comfortingly on the back.

"Can I ask you something?"

Her gaze snapped up from somewhere in the vicinity of his collar, where it parted to reveal a tantalising V of tanned skin, an expanse of skin she found infinitely fascinating for no other reason than what it hinted at.

"Sure."

"You were muttering into your drink earlier. Is everything okay?"

Once again, heat seeped into her cheeks. Could this get

any more embarrassing, the gallant guy having a pity drink with the desperate ditched?

"You know what they say about talking to yourself being the first sign of madness? Well, I'm mad all right. Mad enough to want to throttle my buddy Nigel for bailing on me."

"Ouch." Nate winced and she squared her shoulders, ready to rebuff his pity. Instead, she saw a glimmer of amusement lighting his eyes. "Did he stand you up?"

"Sure did, the jerk. Said he had a better offer from this girl he's been chasing for a while, so he ditches a friend. Nice."

"Very poor form," Nate said, his eyes twinkling beneath a mock frown. "Friends should always come first."

He was making light of her situation and rather than being insulted, laughter bubbled within her at the big deal she'd made out of something pretty insignificant. "Why did you think he stood me up?"

Nate's amusement spread to his mouth as it tilted up at the corners. "Well, if I'd taken one look at that giant bag and the maniacal gleam in your eyes, I would've made a run for it too."

She laughed, surprised the annoyance of being stood up by Nigel had receded, only to be replaced by a surprising need to swap banter with this guy.

"But you didn't make a run for it. You're sitting here."

"Good point." He tipped his glass in her direction before taking a long sip of beer, his gaze never leaving hers.

She couldn't figure him out. He wasn't flirting, making suggestive comments, or hinting at anything untoward, but when he stared at her like that—steady, unwavering, loaded—the air between them sizzled with an invisible current and had her reaching for her drink which she gulped in record time.

"You know it's his loss, right?"

Breaking the hypnotic eye contact, she said, "Yeah, I know. The guy's got his priorities all wrong."

"So he wasn't the love of your life?"

Kristen snorted, unable to picture scruffy, laid-back Nigel as anything other than a colleague she could offload to at the end of a rough day.

"No way. Nigel and I are purely platonic."

"Then he's definitely not worth worrying about now. You can give your friend an earful when you next see him."

"Too right." Considering how trivial her complaint against Nigel was, she wanted to know more about the sadness she'd glimpsed in Nate when she first saw him. "What about you? Any life stories to tell?"

If she'd doused him in her icy drink she would've got the same response: shock combined with pain, sorrow quickly masked by an enforced blank mask.

"Not really. I'm married to my job; don't have time for anything else."

"I know the feeling," she said, trying to cover her monstrous gaff in prying. "So what do you do?"

He hadn't lost his shuttered expression and he waited before speaking as if weighing every word. "I'm involved in the entertainment area too, though on the company side of things."

"So you're one of the corporate bigwigs who control the purse strings, right?"

At last, a glimmer of a smile. "You could say that. I'm the CEO of my own company and apart from handling sporting rights, we branch into other areas too."

"Well, if I ever need a job I'll know who to approach," she said, hating how her mind immediately latched onto his 'handling other areas' and conjuring up startling images of him doing exactly that...with her.

"You do that." He drained his beer and she braced for the inevitable parting, totally confused by her reticence to let him go.

She didn't know this guy.

She didn't want this to end.

She didn't have the foggiest idea what to do.

"I'm hungry after that beer. Do you want to join me for dinner?"

Trying to hide her relief—and elation—she said, "That would be great. The buffet here is the best in Singapore."

"So I've heard. Come on, let's try it."

Sliding off her stool, Kristen ignored her voice of reason yelling 'what do you think you're doing, having dinner with a guy you barely know? Are you nuts?'

"I don't usually do this type of thing," he said, handing her the infamous coat. "Having dinner with women I just met."

"That makes two of us."

Happily ignoring her voice of reason, she sent him a shy smile and fell into step beside him as they headed for the restaurant.

Nate forked a delicious combination of spicy black pepper crab and fried rice into his mouth, trying to concentrate on the amazing food on his plate rather than the intriguing woman sitting across the table from him.

What am I doing here?

He'd asked himself the same question repeatedly over the last half hour and still hadn't come up with an answer. One that made sense, that is. He didn't chat up women, he didn't accept drink invitations, and he sure as hell didn't have dinner with them unless it involved business, yet here he was sharing the best meal he'd had in ages with a beautiful woman he'd known for less than an hour. And enjoying it.

"The food's good?"

He nodded, his gaze fixed on her mouth and the way her lips wrapped around a crab claw, his groin tightening with the sheer eroticism of the movement.

This couldn't be happening. He usually didn't have the time or the inclination. So what was he doing fantasising about this almost-stranger's lush mouth and what it would feel like on him?

"I'm a seafood addict," Kris said, dabbing at her glistening mouth with a serviette while he wrenched his mind out of the gutter. "This place is famous for it."

"Along with the roast duck, tandoori chicken, satays and the million other dishes on offer, you mean?"

She smiled, the power of that one simple action staggering in its ability to capture his interest and keep him riveted. "Wait until you try the desserts."

He didn't have a sweet tooth but at her suggestion he couldn't wait to try a chocolate mousse or lychee sorbet. He'd go along with anything this fascinating woman had to say at the moment, which showed exactly how jet-lagged he must be.

He needed to stop these two day jaunts to Asia if this was the result: a confused, half-drugged state that had him focussing on all the wrong cues, like the way her stunning blue eyes sparkled, how the highlights in her short, layered blonde hair shone, and the way her smile lit up the room.

As for her body—tall, lithe and graceful in the slim pinstripe skirt and pale blue shirt—he'd been struggling not to stare since he'd first seen her hunched over that gigantic bag of hers at the bar with her jacket in a crumple at her feet.

She'd appeared deliciously rumpled and flustered when he'd picked up her coat and nothing like the ice-cool blonde who'd locked gazes with him a minute before with her big sad eyes and grim expression.

He'd watched her for a while—toying with her drink, stabbing at the lemon wedge, her mouth muttering words he couldn't hear. He would've laughed if her expression hadn't been so fragile and though he had his own problems to deal with he'd been unable to walk past her without reaching out and giving her some indication she wasn't alone in the world, some indication he understood.

Boy, did he understand.

People said grief eased with time, that time healed all wounds.

People didn't know jack.

"Dessert is optional. You don't have to try if you'd rather not."

Hating that his mask had slipped for a moment and she must've glimpsed some of what he was feeling, he said, "Sorry, just thinking."

"About something not very pleasant by the looks of it?"

The question hung between them, softly probing but intrusive nonetheless.

"Guess being away from home has me in a mood."

"Being homesick is the pits," she said, placing her serviette on the table and sitting back. "I missed Sydney like crazy when I first came here but you want to know the secret to getting past it?"

"Sure."

Leaning forward, she tapped the side of her nose as if about to depart a secret lost in time. "Orang-utans."

Maybe the jet lag was worse than he thought? He could've sworn she said something obtuse about monkeys.

She nodded, a smile playing about her mouth. "You heard me. Orang-utans. The biggest, goofiest guys on the planet. You can't help but love them. I was feeling pretty lousy my first week here so I took a trip to the Singapore Zoo and spent an hour with the hairy goofballs, having breakfast with them, laughing at their antics. Suddenly, no more homesickness. Instant cure just like that."

She snapped her fingers and he blinked, wondering what it was about this cool yet kooky woman that had him so captivated.

"I'll keep that in mind," he said, shaking his head in disbelief, torn between wanting to bolt from the table before she enthralled him any further and hauling her into his arms to see if she was real.

She flittered between serious and funny, sad and happy, changing emotions like the frenetic activity of the stock market on opening. He hardly knew a thing about her yet he wanted to know more. He didn't know her surname yet he knew she loved seafood, had a brain behind her beauty, and had a thing for big monkeys.

They had little in common yet he knew he didn't want this evening to end.

He wanted to know more. If he were completely honest with himself, he wanted her with a staggering fierceness that clawed at him, begging to be released and soothed by her touch, in her arms, all night.

"Uh-oh, you're having more of those unpleasant thoughts." She picked up the wine bottle and topped up his glass, as if a fine Shiraz would fix what ailed him.

If it were that easy he would've bought out every vineyard in Australia by now.

Direct to the point of bluntness in business, he took a deep breath, opting for the same approach now and hoping it wouldn't earn him a slap.

"Actually, my thoughts aren't so unpleasant."

"Oh?" Her eyebrow kicked up, highlighting the curious glint in her blue eyes.

"I know this is going to sound crazy and you have every right to walk away from this table, but I was thinking we have a connection and I don't want this evening to end."

Surprise flashed across her face, closely followed by indignation? Fear? Hope? He had no idea. It had been a long time since he'd spent this much time with a woman let alone tried to fathom her emotions.

"Are you asking me to spend the night with you?"

He tried not to cringe at her bluntness Looked like he wasn't the only one who favoured the direct approach.

"I don't know what I'm asking," he muttered, eyeing the door and wondering if it was too late to make a run for it. "I don't do this very often. Hell, I haven't been out with a woman for years. But I know one thing. I'm attracted to you. You make me feel good. And I don't want to lose this feeling no matter how temporary."

It was as simple as that. No more, no less. This stunning woman with her expressive eyes and lush mouth had him feeling good for the first time in a long time and he wanted more.

"I think you do know what you're asking," she said, her gaze locked on his, her smile uncertain as she toyed with the ends of the tablecloth, twisting the damask over and over. "I think we both do and my answer is yes."

"Yes?" He exhaled, unaware he'd been holding his breath, filled with elation and anticipation and countless emotions he couldn't describe as she stared at him with excitement glittering in her expressive eyes.

"Yes."

From that moment everything faded into oblivion as he stood, held out his hand and felt an electrifying jolt as she placed hers in it, and led her from the restaurant to the lifts leading up to his room.

They didn't speak.

They didn't need to.

Words seemed superfluous as they entered his room, closed the door and fell into each others arms like two drowning people hanging on to the last life buoy: desperate, frantic, caught up in a storm bigger than the both of them.

As her lips clung to his and he deepened the kiss, his arms sliding around her waist to press her closer, a thrill shot through him.

He'd never done anything so rash, so reckless, so damn impulsive, and it felt good.

It felt great.

Thanks to the beautiful woman in his arms, he realised it was time to start living again.

READ THE GOOD GUY NOW!

FREE BOOK AND MORE

SIGN UP TO NICOLA'S NEWSLETTER for a free book!

Read Nicola's feel-good romance **DID NOT FINISH**

Or her gothic suspense novels **THE RETREAT** and **THE HAVEN**

(The gothic prequel **THE RESIDENCE** is free!)

Try the **CARTWRIGHT BROTHERS** duo

FASCINATION

PERFECTION

The **WORKPLACE LIAISONS** duo

THE BOSS

THE CEO

The **REDEEMING A BAD BOY** series

THE REBEL

THE PLAYER

THE WANDERER

THE CHARMER

THE EX (releasing September 2024)

THE FRIEND (releasing October 2024

Try the **BASHFUL BRIDES** series

NOT THE MARRYING KIND

NOT THE ROMANTIC KIND

NOT THE DARING KIND

NOT THE DATING KIND

The **CREATIVE IN LOVE** series

THE GRUMPY GUY

THE SHY GUY

THE GOOD GUY

Try the **BOMBSHELLS** series

BEFORE (FREE!)

BRASH

BLUSH

BOLD

BAD

BOMBSHELLS BOXED SET

The **WORLD APART** series

WALKING THE LINE (FREE!)

CROSSING THE LINE

TOWING THE LINE

BLURRING THE LINE

WORLD APART BOXED SET

The **HOT ISLAND NIGHTS** duo

WICKED NIGHTS

WANTON NIGHTS

The **ROMANCE CYNICS** duo

CUPID SEASON

SORRY SEASON

The **BOLLYWOOD BILLIONAIRES** series

FAKING IT

MAKING IT

The **LOOKING FOR LOVE** series

LUCKY LOVE

CRAZY LOVE

SAPPHIRES ARE A GUY'S BEST FRIEND

THE SECOND CHANCE GUY

Check out Nicola's website for a full list of her books.

And read her other romances as Nikki North.

'MILLIONAIRE IN THE CITY' series.

LUCKY

FANCY

FLIRTY

FOLLY

MADLY

Check out the **ESCAPE WITH ME** series.

TRUST ME

FORGIVE ME

Try the **LAW BREAKER** series

THE DEAL MAKER

THE CONTRACT BREAKER

About the Author

USA TODAY bestselling and multi-award winning author Nicola Marsh writes page-turning fiction to keep you up all night.

She's published 86 books and sold millions of copies worldwide.

She currently writes contemporary romance and domestic suspense.

She's also a Waldenbooks, Bookscan, Amazon, iBooks and Barnes & Noble bestseller, a RBY (Romantic Book of the Year) and National Readers' Choice Award winner, and a multi-finalist for a number of awards including the Romantic Times Reviewers' Choice Award, HOLT Medallion, Booksellers' Best, Golden Quill, Laurel Wreath, and More than Magic.

A physiotherapist for thirteen years, she now adores writing full time, raising her two dashing young heroes, sharing fine food with family and friends, and her favorite, curling up with a good book!